The Sleepover Club

Hit the Beach!

Have you been invited to all these sleepovers?

The Sleepover Club Best Friends
The Sleepover Club TV Stars
The Sleepover Club Dance-off!
The Sleepover Club Hit the Beach!

Coming soon...

The Sleepover Club Pet Detectives
The Sleepover Club Hey Baby!

The SleePover Club

Hit the Beach!

Harriet Castor

HarperCollins *Children's Books*

The Sleepover Club ® is a registered trademark
of HarperCollins*Publishers* Ltd

First published in Great Britain as *Sleepover Girls go Surfing*
by HarperCollins *Children's Books* in 2003
This edition published by HarperCollins *Children's Books* in 2008
HarperCollins *Children's Books* is a division of HarperCollins*Publishers* Ltd.
77-85 Fulham Palace Road, Hammersmith, London W6 8JB

www.harpercollinschildrensbooks.co.uk

1

Text copyright © Harriet Castor 2003

Original series characters, plotlines and settings © Rose Impey 1997

The author asserts the moral right to be
identified as the author of this work.

ISBN-13 978-0-00-727256-3
ISBN-10 0-00-727256-1

Mixed Sources
Product group from well-managed
forests and other controlled sources
www.fsc.org   Cert no. SW-COC-1806
© 1996 Forest Stewardship Council
FSC

FSC is a non-profit international organisation established to promote the
responsible management of the world's forests. Products carrying the FSC
label are independently certified to assure consumers that they come
from forests that are managed to meet the social, economic and
ecological needs of present and future generations.

Find out more about HarperCollins and the environment at
www.harpercollins.co.uk/green

The Sleepover Kit List

1. Sleeping bag
2. Pillow
3. Pyjamas or a nightdress
4. Slippers
5. Toothbrush, toothpaste, soap etc
6. Towel
7. Teddy
8. A creepy story
9. Food for a midnight feast: chocolate, crisps, sweets, biscuits. Anything you like to eat!
10. Torch
11. Hairbrush
12. Hair bobble or hairband, if you need them
13. Flip flops, sarong and shades
14. A change of clothes
15. Sleepover diary and membership card

Acknowledgement

With major thanks to Kate Trant,
who knows about surfing.
(But any errors are my own.)

Hey, wave warrior! How's it going, dude? Why don't you cruise on over here and hang out with your old buddy Kenny, huh?

No, it's OK, I haven't got sunstroke. It's just my beach speak – I've been practising it ever since we got back from our awesome trip. What's that? You haven't heard about it yet? I can't *believe* one of the others hasn't filled you in – it's all we've been yakking about for ages.

But that's brilliant, cos now I get to tell you!

7

We've been having *the* coolest summer – you're going to be so wowed when you hear about it, I swear. Quick, let's sit over here in the shade so we don't fry. If I get any more sun, I'll be peeling for weeks.

OK, so you remember us all, right? The five super-cool members of the Sleepover Club? First there's me, Kenny. On my birth certificate it says my name's Laura McKenzie, but no one calls me that unless they're narked with me – or they're a teacher. (And the teachers are usually narked with me anyway.)

Next there's Frankie – look, she's over there, flinging a frisbee at Lyndz. Frankie and I have known each other for *ever*, and she's a complete laugh. I think you can blame most of the craziest Sleepover Club ideas on her – life just ain't quiet with Frankie around!

As for Lyndz, she's as mad on ponies as I am on Leicester City Football Club (and that is *seriously* mad). In fact, it's a wonder she's with us right now – usually every spare minute she's got she's off to the stables to shovel horse poo, or whatever it is they make you do down there. (Yeuch!)

Then there's Fliss – Felicity Sidebotham if you're being formal. Yep, that's her, lounging on a towel in her new hot-pink bikini. Summer just has to be her favourite time of year, judging by the number of new outfits she always seems to get. I don't know how she makes it out of the house in the morning. With that many to choose from I'd be dithering till bedtime.

And last – but *so* not least – there's Rosie. Fliss is trying to compare tans with her, but she doesn't look that interested, does she? You might think Rosie's the quietest of the gang. Don't bet on it though, cos sometimes she surprises you. Talk about hidden talents! You won't believe it when I tell you what *she's* been up to.

But I've got to start at the beginning, haven't I? Kenny, get your brain in gear, girl! OK, so here goes.

I know it sounds weird, but the coolest, most glamorous Sleepover adventure yet actually started at Cuddington Primary. Yep, our familiar old school. And it started with those familiar old slime bags, the M&Ms (that's Emily 'the Goblin' Berryman and Emma 'the Queen' Hughes). I'm sure you haven't forgotten about *them* – they're the most stuck-up, snotty girls in our class, and they've been the number one enemies of the Sleepover Club since… well, forever.

It was a Tuesday morning and we were doing Art. Our teacher Mrs Weaver had brought in a packet of balloons, and we were making papier-mâché animals. Sounds weird? I know – but actually it was quite cool. You had to blow up your balloon and then stick your papier-mâché all over it, adding extra bits for legs and ears and whatever.

Frankie and I were doing quite well – even though we'd spent half the lesson flicking bits of gluey paper at each other.

"Mine's not an animal, it's a space rocket," said Frankie, dragging a lump of gunge out of her hair. She had another bit stuck to her forehead, but I wasn't going to let on. It looked hilarious. She peered at my paper-covered balloon. "What's yours?"

"A squashed football?" suggested Fliss.

"Mr Potato Head?" said Rosie.

"Wrong and wrong again," I said. I'd just cut up an egg box and I picked up one of the bits. "Look, this one's the snout," I said. "And these are the little stubby legs. And this one I'll cut in half for the ears. Oink, oink! Any guesses?"

Frankie grinned. "It's Emma Hughes!"

Ha, ha! That made us all fall about.

"I heard my name. Are you talking about me?" said a snooty voice behind us. I spun round and there were the M&Ms – trust them to be listening in! Honestly, it just shows how pathetic they are that they don't have anything else to do but annoy us.

"Yeuch, no," I said, turning back. "That'd be

11

the most boring conversation in the universe."

Then Emily Berryman sniggered. "Did you know you've got paper stuck to your forehead, Frankie?" she said. "You look *so* stupid."

"Yeah, *right*," said Frankie, thinking the Goblin was playing a trick on her. This sent the M&Ms into fits of snorting giggles. Then Frankie put her hand to her forehead and turned bright pink.

Instantly, I was seized with guilt – and the M&Ms' smug faces made my blood boil. "Push off!" I yelled. "Or I'll sit on your stupid balloons and squash them flat!"

The Goblin yelled right back: "You could squash an *elephant* with your big bum!" (See what I mean – brainless or what?)

All the shouting got Mrs Weaver's attention. "What's going on there?" she barked. "Emma and Emily! Get back to your table this instant."

The M&Ms muttered something and shot me a withering look as they stomped back to their places. They're such teacher's pets; they can't stand getting told off for anything. I should've figured they'd start plotting revenge straight away, but I really got into the sticking and gluing after that, so I forgot all about them.

My pig was looking excellent. "When it's dry," I said, holding it up to show the others, "I'm going to paint it blue and yellow." (Leicester City's colours, of course!) "Then I'm going to cut a slot in the top so it's a money box and use it to save up for match tickets and footie mags and stuff. How brilliant is that?"

Nobody got a chance to tell me what a genius I was, though, because right then Mrs Weaver said, "Ten minutes to the bell, everyone. Start clearing up."

Rosie and Lyndz leapt over to the sink to wash up our paint brushes and glue pots. Frankie, Fliss and I picked up all the stray bits of sticky paper. Then we carefully lined up our balloons alongside everyone else's on the shelf above the sink.

Outside at break there was a massive grey cloud hanging over the playground. Soon spits and spots of rain started falling.

"It's supposed to be summer!" said Fliss, scowling up at the sky. "How will I ever get a tan when it's like this?"

"Brrr! I'm going to get my cardie," said Rosie, and she dashed back towards the classroom.

"I think we should go on a summer holiday," said Lyndz. "Sleepover summer camp – wouldn't it be ace? Somewhere hot…"

"We could have midnight feasts under the stars every night," said Frankie.

"Dream on, guys," I said. "Whose parents are going to take all five of us on holiday?"

Just then Rosie came charging towards us, panting and flapping her hands. "Kenny!" she gasped. "Your pig! It's floating in the sink. It's gone all mushy!"

It was obvious from her face that she wasn't joking. I set off for the classroom at supersonic speed. The others followed.

14

Sure enough, when we got there we found the sink half full of water, and bobbing around in it was my Leicester City pig. Or what was left of it. The papier-mâché had turned to gunge and was sliding off the balloon, making the water into gluey soup.

"Nooo!" I fished the slimy balloon out and dumped it on the draining board. "I don't believe it! It's totally ruined!"

"It must've fallen off the shelf," said Rosie gloomily.

"Fallen off?" I said. "No way. I was really careful not to put it near the edge."

"Maybe someone moved it to make room for theirs," suggested Lyndz.

"Uh-huh." I shook my head. "This pig was *pushed*."

By now the bell had rung for the end of break and everyone was piling back into the classroom.

"D'you mean someone did it on purpose?" said Fliss.

Honestly! I'm not saying my friends are thick, but sometimes they're too nice to see what's totally obvious. "Of course they did," I said. "And no prizes for guessing who."

"Settle down, everyone," said Mrs Weaver, striding in with a pile of maths books under her arm.

"I thought it was weird..." began Lyndz as we went back to our seats.

"What?"

"I noticed the M&Ms were at the back of the queue for the sink. Usually they push to the front. They must've let everyone else go first on purpose..."

"Laura, Francesca and Lyndsey – sit down please," said Mrs Weaver.

I growled with frustration and flopped into my chair. A few seats away, the M&Ms were looking at Mrs Weaver with wide-eyed innocent expressions, like two puppies on a TV advert. This is it, I thought. A pig too far. This means Kenny on the warpath. Chaaaaarge!

16

If I'd known what was going to happen, there's no way I would have done it, would I? I just wish someone had turned me into Mystic Kenny for the day, and kitted me out with a crystal ball.

No such luck. Instead, I spent the whole of the maths lesson racking my brain, trying to come up with a brilliant revenge plan. Frankie kept passing me little scribbled drawings of pigs called Emily and Emma to cheer me up. They made me giggle all right, but by lunchtime, though I was feeling happier, I still hadn't had any ideas.

Then, when we were sitting in the dining hall eating our packed lunches, I had a flash of inspiration.

"Don't you want that yoghurt, Fliss?" I said.

"Urgh, no." She pushed it away from her. "Andy did the shopping and he forgot to get low-fat again." (Andy is Fliss's mum's boyfriend. He's really nice.)

"Fliss!" Lyndz laughed. "One yoghurt isn't going to make you fat!"

Fliss wrinkled her nose. "I don't like the taste if I know it's not low-fat."

"Can I have it, then?" I said.

"If you want."

I didn't eat it – I slipped it into my lunch box. I had *the* best plan.

When we'd finished, we headed back to the classroom as usual to dump our lunch stuff. I hung back, pretending to look for something in my rucksack.

"Come on, slowcoach!" said Lyndz, standing at the door.

"You go ahead – I'll catch you up," I said. When she'd gone, I hurried over to Emily Berryman's desk. Her bag was on her chair. Quickly, I unzipped it. Inside was a jumble of books and games kit – she's not very neat.

I took Fliss's yoghurt and tweaked the lid back about halfway. Then I buried the pot deep in the bag.

 18

When I got out to the playground, I must've looked pleased with myself, because Frankie said, "Hey, Mystery Queen – have you been up to something?"

"Maybe." I wiggled my eyebrows. "You'll find out." It was going to be the funniest surprise ever.

Back in the classroom at the end of the lunch break, Emily picked up her bag and dumped it on the floor, but didn't open it. I was hoping she'd shake it around a bit – that would really get the yoghurt slopping – but no such luck. Anyway, I was soon thinking about other things, because Mrs Weaver came in clutching a stack of envelopes and started handing them out. They were addressed to our parents.

"Hey, what's this?" said Lyndz, holding hers up to the light in the hope that it was see-through. Sealed letters to take home always give us the jitters.

"Something boring, I bet," said Fliss. "PTA meeting. Or a sponsored spell."

We all groaned.

"Quiet now, everyone," said Mrs Weaver, clapping her hands. "I have something exciting to tell you. The letters that I've just handed out are to inform your parents about this year's summer trip."

That made us sit up and take notice. "Please let it be Alton Towers," muttered Frankie next to me. "Or the London Eye – that would be wicked!"

"You're a very lucky class," said Mrs Weaver. "This trip is really something special – it's an activity week on the north Devon coast."

Oh. My. Gosh. Frankie and I clutched each other. A week? A whole *week*? This was awesome!

"Is it by the sea, with a beach?" Danny McCloud called out.

Mrs Weaver smiled. "Yes, by the sea with a beach, Danny. But we won't just be sunbathing all day. There'll be a variety of activities to choose from, and we'll be staying in a youth hostel, where we'll all get involved with the cooking and cleaning. It's about co-operation and working together as well as having fun together."

I don't really think anyone in the class had taken in a word since "sea" and "beach". I looked round at Lyndz, Rosie and Fliss and we did a big thumbs up. "It's our dream of a Sleepover Club summer camp – come true!" squeaked Rosie.

Everyone was chattering excitedly. "Settle down, now," said Mrs Weaver. "Obviously, your parents will need to agree to it. In your envelopes there's a form for them to sign and you'll need to bring it back with a deposit. BUT – " she looked round seriously " – no one's place on this trip is guaranteed. Each of you will need to prove to me that you can behave responsibly. Any misbehaviour may affect your chances of going."

Yeah yeah, I was thinking. Usual teacher guff about good behaviour. We'd just have to make sure we didn't get into any serious trouble between now and… Then it struck me.

Right at this moment there was a leaky yoghurt pot, sitting in Emily Berryman's bag like a time bomb.

There was only one thing for it: I had to get the yoghurt back. And fast.

When she'd finished talking about the school trip, Mrs Weaver said, "Now, we'd better get on with our history lesson, hadn't we? We're going to start a new topic today: Henry VIII and His Six Wives. Who would like to fetch the books from the cupboard for me and give them out?"

As you probably know, I'm not usually the world's keenest volunteer. Not unless someone's giving out Leicester City tickets as rewards! But today I shot my hand up faster than a goalie making the save of his life.

Even Mrs Weaver looked surprised. "Thank you, Laura," she said. As I clambered out of my seat, I hissed to Frankie, "When I get to the Goblin's desk, distract her!"

"What?" Frankie looked confused. "How? Why?"

But I didn't have time to explain. I fetched the pile of books and sailed round the room handing them out, one between two. When I got near Emily I winked at Frankie; she tugged Emily's sleeve and waved her exercise book in front of her nose, saying could she copy her notes on the Egyptians and did she have that stuff about Cleopatra from last week? I think Emily honestly thought Frankie had gone stark raving bonkers – and I don't blame her. I took my chance, though – I bent down to Emily's bag and had just got my fingers on the zip when I heard Mrs Weaver's voice saying, "Laura, what *are* you doing?"

I snapped upright again. "Nothing, Mrs Weaver."

Well, after that I spent the whole lesson feeling like I had ants in my pants. I couldn't concentrate, couldn't think of anything except the Yoghurt Pot of Doom. If only I could've made myself invisible for just two minutes, I could've sorted everything out, no problem. It was sooo frustrating.

Our last lesson of the day was P.E. In the girls' changing room, everyone was excited, talking about the school trip. I was so busy imagining just how ace it was going to be that for a few moments I forgot all about Emily and the yoghurt pot.

"D'you reckon there'll be donkey rides on the sands?" said Lyndz, sitting down to unbuckle her shoes. "I saw seals on a beach in Scotland once!" (Lyndz is animal mad, in case you hadn't noticed.)

"Devon's a long way from Scotland," laughed Rosie.

"I *know*. But seals live in other places too."

Frankie grinned. "I bet Fliss is wondering whether there'll be hunky lifeguards on the beach."

"Am not!" said Fliss from inside her games t-shirt. But when she pulled it over her head she'd turned bright pink.

Suddenly, there was a piercing shriek. "Aieeee!"

All around us the excited chattering stopped dead. I spun round to see Emily Berryman holding up a yellow t-shirt. It looked as if Frankie's baby sister Izzy had been sick all down the front.

Emily dropped the t-shirt on the floor and started pulling more and more things out of her bag, all of them slimed with yoghurt. A sock, an exercise book, her games shorts...

"Gross! Look at her trainers!" By now, practically everyone in the room was shrieking with laughter. Next to me, Frankie and Rosie were giggling fit to burst, and Lyndz had already got hiccups. Fliss, though, was wincing – I reckon she was imagining how upset she'd be if someone messed with *her* clothes.

The next minute the changing room door swung open. It was Mrs Weaver and she didn't look pleased. "Girls! What on earth is all this racket?"

"Mrs Weaver, Emily's spilt a yoghurt in her bag."

Mrs Weaver sighed and marched over to Emily. She wrinkled her nose when she saw the state of her things. "For goodness' sake, Emily. You should keep your lunch more carefully."

"But, Mrs Weaver!" Emily looked like she was about to cry. "It's not *my* lunch. I didn't have a yoghurt. Someone put it in my bag on purpose!"

There was a moment's silence. I could almost hear Mrs Weaver's brain whirring. Then – guess who was the first "someone" that popped into her head? Who had she spotted fiddling with Emily's bag?

Lyndz nudged me. "Why's Weaver loo-hic-king at you?" she whispered.

But before I could answer, Mrs Weaver snapped, "Laura. Go and wait for me outside Mrs Poole's office. Now!"

27

Man oh man. How can a load of teachers get so massively, crazily angry about one measly little yoghurt, for goodness' sake? It was going to wash out of Emily's games kit, no problem. And OK, her geography book was a bit slimy, but to be honest she's not the world's best brain at geography anyhow. She'd have been better off copying Emma's notes in the first place, I reckon.

But that didn't seem to be the point. Mrs Poole, our headteacher, went really po-faced and stony when Mrs Weaver explained what had happened.

"I cannot understand how you can be so utterly irresponsible, Laura," she said, peering at me over the top of her glasses like I was some horrid insect she wanted to squash. "Not to mention so disrespectful of other people's property. Did you think it was *funny*?"

Why do teachers always ask that? Dur! Of

course I thought it was funny or I wouldn't have done it, would I? But I couldn't say that.

"No, Mrs Poole," I muttered, looking at my shoes.

"How would you like it if someone covered your belongings in yoghurt?"

Blah blah blah. I tried to tell her what had happened to my pig but she wouldn't listen. She just went on and on. By the time she'd finished droning it was home time, and I felt like one of Henry VIII's wives who'd been sent to the Tower.

I headed back to the classroom in a daze. There I found Lyndz, Rosie, Fliss and Frankie, sitting in a huddle with their coats on. They sprang off the desks when they saw me and clustered round.

"Was that really what you did with my yoghurt?" asked Fliss, giggling.

"Ace plan, Kenco!" said Frankie, putting her hand up for high fives. "Serves the Goblin right after what they did to your pig!"

"Kenny – are you OK?" said Lyndz, peering at me. "You look a bit sick."

"I feel majorly sick," I said. Lyndz took a step back. I reckon she thought I was going to barf on her shoes right then and there!

"Pooley didn't make a massive deal of it, did she?" asked Rosie.

"Course not," said Frankie. "She's a pushover!" Frankie's right – usually Pooley's nice, and much softer than Weaver.

But this time it was different. My nightmare had come true. "She made the most gigantic, humungous deal of it you can imagine," I said, slumping into my chair and looking round at my friends. "I'm sorry, guys. I can't go on the school trip."

You know when someone gives you something, and then snatches it away the very next minute – it's so much worse than if you'd never had it in the first place, isn't it?

At that moment, I wished I'd never heard about the trip. Even better, I wished I'd never set eyes on Emily Berryman and her horrid bag in my life.

My friends were all just standing there, opening and shutting their mouths like goldfish. They couldn't believe what'd happened. Well, that made five of us.

I got up and started stuffing my things angrily into my rucksack. "If you hadn't been so picky about your yoghurt, Fliss, I never would've got into this mess," I said.

"Hey!" Fliss protested. "It wasn't my fault! It was your stupid idea…"

"Stop it!" yelled Frankie. Then, more quietly, she said, "It was the M&Ms' fault for ruining Kenny's pig in the first place. Come on, guys – we'd better get going."

We all grabbed our bags and headed out of the classroom.

As we were crossing the playground I dodged round Frankie so I could walk next to Fliss. "Look, I didn't mean it back there," I said. "I'm sorry."

"It's OK." Fliss nodded. "I'd be really upset too if I were you."

31

Just then Lyndz bounced up behind us and flung her arms round me. "It's not fair!" she wailed, squeezing me really tight. "It won't be a proper Sleepover Club trip without Kenny!"

"Too right it won't!" I said. I know it's really mean, but I couldn't bear the thought that they'd all be going on this fabulous holiday without me. "Hey..." I stopped in my tracks – the others stopped too. "Maybe the Sleepover Club should boycott the trip – you know, as a protest?" I said. "If one of us stays home, we all stay home!"

There was a silence. "Er... maybe," said Lyndz.

"Oh, forget it," I said grumpily. "I'll be fine. Send me a postcard, guys." And I stomped off.

It's not like me to get down about things, but that night I was a real misery-guts. I think Mum and Dad presumed I'd had a row with my sister Molly – a good guess, since she's about as annoying as they come and having to share a bedroom with her is torture. I didn't want to tell them what had happened at school, because I couldn't bear another lecture, and anyway I knew Molly would be all sarky and superior about it. Why does anyone think having sisters is a nice thing?

When I woke up the next morning, I felt fine – for about five minutes. Then I remembered everything and my heart sank with this awful *whump*. I didn't want to go to school and have to listen to people talking about Devon all day and how cool it was going to be.

But I had no choice (if your dad's a doctor, like mine, pretending to be sick *never* gets you the day off school).

I'd just walked in through the school gate when I saw the freakiest thing. You'll laugh, I know, but I had to sit down on one of the playground benches, because I honestly thought I was having a funny turn.

What I saw was this: Frankie talking to Emily

Berryman. They were actually having a conversation. Neither of them looked like they were enjoying it much, it's true, but they weren't yelling or pinching each other or taking the mickey.

"All right, Kenny?" said Lyndz, bounding up to me.

"What's going on?" I said, pointing at Frankie.

"Oh that," said Lyndz, all breezy like it wasn't strange at all. "Just a Sleepover Club plan."

I looked at her. "What do you mean? How come I don't know about it? I'm in the Sleepover Club!" A horrible thought – that they'd thrown me out for being grumpy yesterday – shot into my brain. "Aren't I?"

"Course you are," laughed Lyndz. "Don't worry. The rest of us talked on the phone last night and decided we had to do something to help, that's all."

I didn't have a clue what to say – and that's a rarity for loudmouth McKenzie, I can tell you. I didn't much like the idea that Frankie, Lyndz, Rosie and Fliss had been talking last night and

34

had left me out of it. On the other hand, I felt a whole heap better knowing that my friends were on the case.

"So – spill. What's the plan?" I said.

"Ask Frankie," said Lyndz. And before I could grab her and threaten her with a Chinese burn, she'd dashed off.

So I legged it across the playground towards Frankie, but as I passed the window of Mrs Poole's office, I slammed on the brakes and did a major double take. It couldn't be… it was! Fliss and Rosie were in there, talking to Mrs Poole. What on earth was going on?

This was seriously weird. Shaking my head, I set off again. By now, Frankie had finished her cosy chat with the Goblin.

"What's going on, Frankie Thomas?" I demanded, grabbing her round her middle. "Tell me, or I'll tickle you till you wee yourself!"

"Aaaagh! Ah-ah-ah, noooo!" Even when she's doubled up with giggles, Frankie's a good match for anyone. With one nifty move, she twisted out of my grip and leapt away, laughing. "You'll find out, Sherlock! We've got a plan. It may not work, though…"

Just then the bell rang.

What could I do? Short of biffing Frankie with my rucksack (and I was in enough trouble anyway, thank you very much), I couldn't think of a thing. So I tramped inside along with everyone else and sat there like a lemon while Mrs Weaver took the register. Just as she got to the Ts there was a knock on the classroom door. It was Mrs Lynch, the seriously scary school secretary.

"I'm so sorry to disturb you, Mrs Weaver," she said, "but could you spare Emily Berryman for a moment? Mrs Poole would like to see her."

"Of course," said Mrs Weaver, looking surprised. "Run along, Emily."

Though Mrs Weaver looked surprised, the Goblin didn't. She shot Frankie a look I couldn't fathom, and followed Mrs Lynch out of the room.

I have to say, when Emily came back ten minutes later and said to Mrs Weaver that now old Pooley wanted to see *me*, I was past being surprised. Mrs Poole could have walked in with a blancmange elephant on her head and I wouldn't have batted an eyelid (though I might have fallen off my chair laughing).

As I stood up, Frankie squeezed my hand. "Good luck," she whispered. Good luck with what? I wondered. Was I going to be carted off to the Tower of London after all?

When I reached her office, though, I found Mrs Poole looking a lot jollier than the day before.

"Some more facts have come to light about yesterday's unfortunate incident with the yoghurt, Laura," she said. "I understand that there had been some provocation."

"Yes, Mrs Poole," I began. "I tried to tell you…"

But Mrs Poole held up her hand. "Emily admitted to me that she and Emma ruined your papier-mâché project. However, this was no excuse for what you did. If someone behaves badly, you only bring yourself down to their level by retaliating – do you understand?"

I nodded.

"Still, I do see that in the circumstances, banning you alone from the Devon activity week seems unfair." Mrs Poole frowned. "I could of course make you, Emma and Emily all stay behind…"

Aaargh! The thought of having a week alone with the M&Ms was so hideous it made me feel dizzy.

Luckily, Mrs Poole quickly went on, "…but some of your classmates made an appeal to me this morning, saying that they wouldn't enjoy the trip without you. How lovely to have such loyal friends, Laura!"

I nodded again as a big grin crept over my face. Way to go, Sleepover Club!

"So – as long as Mrs Weaver and I can find no fault whatsoever with your behaviour during the next three weeks," said Mrs Poole, "I've decided that you can go to Devon."

I could have hugged her. I could have danced around her office and turned cartwheels right down the corridor. Instead, I managed to squeak, "Thanks, Mrs Poole!"

When I got out, my friends were waiting for me: four eager faces, looking hopeful and excited.

"Well?" said Frankie.

"She said I can go!"

"Yeeesssss!"

For ages we were one big jumping, hugging bundle. Then I did high fives with everyone in turn. "Thank you sooo much, guys," I said. "I owe you, big time!"

"Well, we couldn't really go without you, could we?" said Rosie.

"Not if it was going to make you so grumpy!" laughed Lyndz.

"I can't believe it," I said, shaking my head. "It's going to be the most awesome week ever!"

"Swimming in the sea!" said Rosie, bouncing up and down.

"Donkey rides!" said Lyndz.

Fliss clapped her hands. "I'll have to buy a new sunhat!"

"Only one?" laughed Frankie.

"Hey, Frankie," I said a moment later, as we headed out to the playground for break. "How did you get Emily to admit it?"

Frankie grinned. "I told her the school'd had hidden CCTV cameras fitted in the classrooms at half term – you know, like they have in shops to catch thieves."

I gasped. "No! Seriously?"

Frankie nodded. "I said Pooley had seen the tape, but she was waiting for them to own up." She giggled. "I can't believe she fell for it!"

"I have seriously *got* to keep away from the M&Ms now," I said. "If you see me going within a hundred miles of them, grab me."

"Don't worry," said Frankie. "I'll lock you in the stationery cupboard if I have to. And once we get to Devon, even if they're being totally annoying, I reckon there's going to be loads to take our minds off them."

And boy, was she right about *that* one!

"Sit down, everyone, so I can count you!"

Mrs Weaver had to yell above the noise. The whole class had piled on to the coach in a MEGA excited mood and people were bouncing up and down so much the coach was actually rocking.

"I've got buttons!" said Rosie, waving a bag of chocolates.

"I've got Pringles!" said Lyndz.

Fliss knelt up in her seat. "I only packed four

42

swimming costumes. Do you think that'll be enough?"

"Fliss!" I yelped. "The rest of us only *own* one! How many does a girl need?"

As the coach pulled away we all waved like mad things. It's funny – if I'd been going somewhere on my own for a week, I would've felt sad saying goodbye to Mum and Dad. But heading off with my friends didn't worry me at all – I couldn't wait for our majorly wicked holiday to begin.

There was only our class on the trip, but we had three teachers with us: Mrs Weaver (of course), Miss Walsh who usually teaches Year 5, and Mrs Daniels who usually teaches Year 4. They were sitting at the front near the driver, miles away from us, thank goodness.

Frankie was next to me, Rosie and Fliss had the seats behind us, and Lyndz had a double-seat all to herself across the gangway. Now Rosie stuck her face in the gap between our headrests. "Which first, guys – magazine or choccies?" She was flapping a copy of *Mizz*, one of those really girlie mags that are filled with things about hair and make-up. Yawn! Luckily, I'd brought the latest Leicester City fanzine, so I pulled that out of my rucksack.

"I brought a puzzle book but it's in my suitcase," said Lyndz. Our suitcases were packed in a big compartment at the bottom of the coach.

As it turned out, though, we were far too excited to settle to reading anything. Instead, we played I-spy and scissors-paper-stone and took turns at trying on Fliss's new sunglasses.

"Andy says they make me look like a film star," said Fliss.

"Who? Tom Cruise?" I said, and she boffed me with the magazine.

It was a seriously long journey. After a few hours, we stopped at a picnic area and ate our sandwiches. Then it was back on to the stuffy coach. Frankie asked if the driver could put his radio on, and he said yes – way cool! When Will Young came on all the girls sang along (yep, even me!) while all the boys made sicky noises. It was hilarious.

"I can see the sea!"

Simon Baxter had been saying that for hours, every time there was something sparkly in the distance. The first time he said it we hadn't even left Leicestershire, I reckon, which is about as far from the sea as you can get.

This time, though, Frankie nudged me in the ribs. "Hey – he's right!" she said, jabbing her finger on the window.

Suddenly, I was awake. Seeing the sea was always going to be exciting, but after hours and hours of boring motorways it was like a dream come true. It was only a shimmering strip on the horizon at first, but it got wider and wider as the road wound nearer to the water.

"Can't they stop the coach so we can jump in right now?" sighed Lyndz.

"I can see people swimming!" said Rosie.

"Hey…" I pointed. "Isn't that guy on the beach carrying a surfboard? Coo-*ell*!"

The road followed the edge of the sands for a while and then turned to the right, passing a sign saying "Welcome to Rawnston" and heading on through the little town. We still had our noses pressed to the window, and we saw loads of really cool-looking cafés with teenagers hanging around outside, dressed in excellent beach gear.

"They are seriously stylish," said Frankie.

"We have *got* to check out the clothes shops here," said Fliss. "I knew I should've brought more spending money." Frankie and I rolled our eyes. Knowing Fliss, she probably had three times more than the rest of us anyway.

I flung the window open. "Oh wow – you can smell the sea!"

It was ten minutes later and we were bouncing around our room at the Beach Road Hostel. Thanks to Fliss, we'd managed to bag the only room in the house with five beds –

two sets of bunks and one single. (Her case had been so heavy the coach driver'd had to carry it in, leaving her free to dash round and find the best room. Result!)

Frankie was the last to arrive. "Sleepover Club HQ!" she yelled, plonking her case down and punching the air. "Hey – bags I get a top bunk!"

"Me too!" I said, racing over from the window and clambering up one of the ladders. Rosie dashed for the bunk beneath me and Lyndz grabbed the one below Frankie.

Fliss was left standing in the middle of the room. She shrugged. "I don't like bunk beds anyway," she said. "If I'm on a top bunk, I always think I'm going to fall out. And if I'm on the bottom, I think it's going to collapse on me."

"Oh thanks," said Lyndz. "I hadn't thought of that."

"All right in here?" Mrs Weaver popped her head round the door.

"Yes, Mrs Weaver!" we chorused.

"Come down to the dining room at six o'clock.

47

We're going to explain how things will work this week and then we'll have dinner. OK?"

The dining room was a bit like the one at school, with long tables and benches instead of chairs. When we went in, the teachers were standing at the front with an older boy and girl who looked just like the teenagers we'd seen hanging around the cafés in town.

"Who're they?" hissed Rosie as we squashed together on one of the benches.

None of us had a clue. They both looked a bit grungy but really cool. They were tanned and their hair looked like they spent loads of time in the sun. The boy was wearing baggy shorts and a funky t-shirt, and the girl had on a short dress with cut-off leggings underneath. That probably sounds weird, but it looked really brilliant. She wore lots of bead bracelets and there were colours threaded through her hair.

"I'm Bethany and this is Aidan," said the girl when everyone had sat down. "And we're your Team Leaders for the week."

48

"That means we'll be helping with some of your activities," said Aidan, "and we'll be organising you into teams to take it in turns to cook dinner and wash up and stuff."

You might've expected everyone to moan at the idea of washing up, but no one did. I reckon they thought even *that* would be cool with Bethany and Aidan.

"After dinner a choice of activities will be put up on the noticeboard," said Miss Walsh. "When you've decided what you want to do, just write your name on the relevant list. The teams for cooking will be up on the board too. But tonight – since it's our first night – Bethany and Aidan have kindly cooked for us!"

Everyone whooped and clapped at that. Bethany and Aidan went off to the kitchen and came back with enormous bowls of pasta and salad, which they passed round so that everyone could help themselves. I nudged Frankie and pointed at Fliss. She was watching Aidan with this dreamy, far-away expression on her face.

49

"Fliss is in *lurve!*" we said together and fell about laughing.

After dinner there was a big crush round the noticeboard as everyone tried to see the activity lists.

"There's, er… beach volleyball," said Frankie, standing on tiptoe. "And pony-trekking."

"Ace!" said Lyndz.

"And… wait a sec… surfing."

"Excellent!" I looked round at the others. "I vote for surfing. Definitely."

Have you ever tried it? We did it once in Spain and it was totally brilliant, though I remember swallowing quite a lot of water.

"Surfing's really tricky," Fliss said, frowning. "In Spain we all fell off the whole time."

"I know, but it was ace fun," I said. "And we'll get better at it, won't we?"

"I want to do a pony-trek," said Lyndz.

"But that's the stuff you do at home, Lyndz!" said Frankie.

Lyndz shook her head. "The countryside's

50

different round here, and the ponies will be different too."

"Oh, but Lyndz..." I tugged at her sleeve in a pleading kind of way. "You can't come to the seaside and then not do anything on the beach."

Rosie said quickly, "Look. The notice says there's another pony-trek later in the week. So why don't we try surfing first, then sign up for a trek later?"

"OK." Lyndz nodded.

Phew! I didn't want us to have a barney on our first day.

"Well, *I* think we should do volleyball," said Fliss firmly.

Aaargh!

Just then we heard a voice behind us. "All right, guys?" It was Aidan. He grinned. "Found something you're interested in?"

Fliss just stared up at him like a love-struck puppy (it was dead embarrassing), but luckily Frankie jumped in and said, "We're thinking of surfing, but we're not sure..."

Aidan nodded and looked over his shoulder. Then he said, "I'm not supposed to tell you this, but that's the one I'd go for. Surfing is a total buzz. You'll love it."

Excellent! It was all I could do not to make a complete wally of myself and hug him.

"Do you surf, then?" asked Rosie.

Aidan nodded. "That's why Bethany and I are here," he said. "We've come to Rawnston for the summer to catch some waves – we're just working at the hostel to pay for the surf-time."

When he'd gone, I looked at Fliss. She pursed her lips, thinking. "I reckon maybe we should do the surfing," she said. And we all burst out laughing.

What with the coach journey and all the excitement we were totally cream-crackered. We'd planned to switch our torches on after lights out and tell one another stories, but even before Mrs Daniels came round to check we were in bed, everyone was yawning so much it looked like a major fly-catching competition.

"We've got to plan our midnight feast," said Rosie sleepily.

"Do you reckon Aidan will be our surfing teacher?" came Fliss's voice through the dark.

Everyone giggled.

"Goodnight, guys," said Frankie.

"Night," I mumbled dozily. "This week… it's going to be amazing."

And I was right. But you know what? I would never in a million years have guessed just *how* amazing it was going to turn out to be.

The next morning, we woke up to blue skies and sunshine. "Perfect beach weather!" squealed Fliss, leaping out of bed and twirling round the room. It was all the rest of us could do to stop her going down to breakfast in her bikini and sunglasses.

I pulled on my favourite Leicester City shirt and my comfiest shorts and flip-flops, and raced Frankie down the stairs. On breakfast duty this morning was the M&Ms' team.

"What d'you reckon it'll be – slugs on toast?" I said as we all clambered into our bench seats.

"Yeurgh!" said Lyndz. "You're making me feel sick!"

In fact, breakfast turned out to be surprisingly normal. There was a choice of cornflakes or muesli and then toast. The team, helped by Aidan, had made fried bananas too, which looked weird – brown and squidgy – but tasted really good. I reckon Lyndz ate about four of them.

After breakfast we had to get ready for our activities. Not a single person, it turned out, had signed up for pony-trekking – I guess because no one could bear to miss out on the beach on our first day.

"Don't forget your sunscreen, everyone!" called out Mrs Weaver.

The beach was only a shortish walk from our hostel, so we set off in a long straggly crocodile, with Bethany and Aidan leading the way, and the teachers at the back making sure no one got lost.

"Hey, where did you get those flip-flops, Fliss?" said Rosie. "They're so cool!"

I think Fliss had changed about three times that morning already – she wasn't sure which of her 'beach outfits' to wear first. Now she had on a lime-green t-shirt and a bright pink sarong, and her flip-flops were matching pink, with an enormous fabric flower over the bit that goes between your toes.

"I think Aidan will like those flip-flops," I said, winking at Frankie, who was walking next to me.

"Definitely – oh and Fliss," said Frankie loudly, "did you see on the list that Ryan Scott's signed up for surfing too?"

Ryan Scott's this boy in our class that Fliss has a thing about (yep, she's seriously weird). Fliss just turned round and stuck her tongue out at us, but she wasn't really cross – we were all too excited for that.

The minute we got to the beach, everyone kicked off their shoes – including the teachers.

There's nothing like the feeling of warm sand under your bare feet, is there? The way you can squidge your toes down, squiggle them right into the sand – bliss!

"OK," said Aidan, "everyone who signed up for beach volleyball – you're with me."

"Boo," muttered Fliss.

"And all the surfers – come this way," said Bethany.

The teachers split up too – Mrs Weaver and Mrs Daniels went with the volleyball group, and Miss Walsh came with us, as we followed Bethany to a different part of the beach.

"D'you think the water'll be cold?" said Lyndz.

"Are you joking?" I squinted skywards. The sun was pretty baking, and there were just a couple of tiny fluffy white clouds.

"But sometimes the water takes ages to heat up," said Lyndz. I think maybe she was still wishing we were doing the pony- trekking, but I was so pleased we'd persuaded her – this was going to be ace!

At last, Bethany stopped near a beach hut, put her bag down on the sand and turned to us. "This area of the beach is reserved for learner surfers," she explained. "It's important you don't get tangled up with people who are trying to swim. And believe me, you don't want to be on the same patch as the surfers who think they know it all, either!"

She gestured over her shoulder. Quite a long way further down the beach, I could see a load of people on the sand carrying surfboards under their arms, and more of them bobbing about in the water.

Bethany fished in her pocket and pulled out some keys. Then she unlocked the beach hut and called, "Any volunteers to help me get the gear out?" In a spray of sand, Frankie and I dashed over.

"Cheers, girls," said Bethany, giving us a grin.

Inside the hut there was a big stack of yellow and blue boards. "Hey, Leicester City surfboards!" I said, nudging Frankie in the ribs.

"Saddo," she mouthed, laughing at me.

"They all need to come out," said Bethany, nodding towards the boards. "I'll bring the rest."

Outside, the boys were already kicking sand at each other, and Fliss had stretched out for a quick spot of sunbathing. As I brought out the last of the boards, I heard Bethany behind me say, "Well, *you* took your time."

I turned round. There was a boy about Bethany's age leaning against the door of the hut as if he'd been there for hours. And – I kid you not – he looked *exactly* like Brad Pitt. It was spooky.

As Frankie and I went back to sit with the others, I could see Lyndz and Rosie nudging each other. Fliss still had her eyes shut.

"Maybe it *is* Brad Pitt," Rosie was saying. "Maybe he flew over to see Madonna now that she lives in London, and he thought while he's here he'd come and check out the beach life..."

"Wait till Fliss sees him," giggled Lyndz. "She'll never look at Aidan again!"

"What? Who?" murmured Fliss, sitting up.

"Everyone – this is Jude," said Bethany, raising her voice. "He's going to be teaching surfing today, along with me. We'll split you into two groups…" Quickly, Frankie, Lyndz, Rosie and I huddled together as Bethany waved her arm, cutting an imaginary line down the middle of where everyone was sitting.

"You'll be my lot," she added, looking at our half. Phew! We were all together! Then Bethany turned to the others, "And you're Jude's group, OK?"

"Fliss, what're you doing?" hissed Lyndz.

"The dividing line was, like, *here*," said Fliss, waving her arm between her and the rest of us. "So I must be in Jude's group." She looked pained. "It's a *real* shame that I'm not with you guys, though…"

I caught hold of her sarong and yanked her back over to us. "Just cos he looks like Brad Pitt you're not splitting up the Sleepover Club," I said.

Fliss went pink and scowled at me, like I was

a major spoilsport. But I mean, come on –
loyalties or what?

It turned out we'd all had a narrow escape.
Jude seemed really grumpy as he trudged a
little way off with his group and started
explaining to them what they were going to
do. It looked like he'd prefer to be anywhere in
the world rather than on Rawnston beach
with a load of Cuddington Primary pupils.

"Well, he's a bundle of laughs – *not*," said
Frankie.

"And why does he keep shooting Bethany
such dirty looks?" added Rosie.

"Because she's just obviously massively
better and cooler than he is," I said.

And Bethany *was* cool. She was really fun –
cheerful and friendly, and she didn't talk down
to us like we were five year olds, either.

Our group was just the Sleepover Club, plus
Alana 'Banana' Palmer. She's a bit of a drip and
she often hangs around with the M&Ms – which
shows she's got no taste. Sometimes, they're

quite horrible to her too – she must be crazy!

Anyhow, we didn't much mind having her in our group, though of course it would've been cooler if the Sleepover Club had had Bethany all to ourselves.

"Right – I just want to check that you're all strong swimmers, yes?" said Bethany. "It's really important that you tell me if you're not." She looked round at each of us.

A while ago Rosie would have had to stick her hand up. I don't know if you remember when we did that swimathon at Cuddington Baths? We found out then that Rosie couldn't swim at all. After that, she started having lessons, though, and before we knew it she'd turned into a total mermaid! She's the strongest swimmer of us all now, I reckon.

Anyway, next Bethany told us a bit of general stuff about surfing. About how the idea, for a beginner at least, was to wade out into the water, waist- or chest-deep, turn round, wait for a wave, then lie on your board and let the wave shoot you back in to the beach.

"What you'll see the other guys doing down there…" she nodded further down the sands "…is putting their boards at an angle to the beach and surfing *across* the face of the wave as it comes in. Ignore them – that's advanced stuff. We're just going to stick to the little waves for now and the simple moves, OK?"

We all nodded. But it looked like it was going to be a while before we even got to go in the water. First, Bethany wanted us to practise our positions on our boards – on the sand.

"The hardest thing at the beginning is learning how to balance on the board," she said. "You'll start off lying on your tummy – that's quite straightforward. Then we'll practise getting to a kneeling position. And then we'll try standing. Don't worry if it takes you a while – there's a kind of knack to it. It might be frustrating at first, but all of a sudden, you'll just get it. And then it'll feel brilliant."

"Oh no," groaned Rosie. "I'm going to spend the entire week falling in, I just know it."

Bethany told us to find a level bit of sand to put our boards on. Because each board had a little fin on the bottom, you had to dig a hole in the sand before it could lie flat. Then, because the underside was slightly curved, you had to pack some sand in round the edges of the board to stop it rocking. What a palaver, as my gran would say!

"Now, lie on your tummy with your toes on the end of the board," instructed Bethany. "In this position, you can use your arms to paddle, or if you're letting a wave bring you in to the beach, you can grip the sides of the board."

I hoped none of the expert surfers was watching us. "Hey," I muttered, "anyone else feel stupid doing this or is it just me?"

"Now push on your arms and bring your legs under you, so that you're kneeling," said Bethany. "Sit back on your heels – that's right."

"This is so cool!" said Fliss. "It's like a weird dance routine!"

"When you've had a bit of practice, you can slide your feet in and go straight to standing, like this," said Bethany. She lay on the sand, pushed up on her arms and brought her feet under her in a crouching position, then stood up. "Your feet should be turned to the side, see, one in front of the other. Keep your knees slightly bent to help you balance."

"Wheee!" said Lyndz, pretending she was zipping through the water.

"We'll never do this in a million years," moaned Rosie.

Frankie was busy doing silly dancing on her board, holding her nose and sticking her other hand up in the air, and squiggling downwards like she was shimmying underwater.

"Good!" said Bethany, who was looking the other way, watching Alana. "OK, then – two more pieces of equipment before we get wet." She delved into a box she'd brought out of the beach hut. "First, we all need to wear one of these." She was holding up a couple of padded sleeveless jackets in neon orange and yellow.

"Are they life jackets?" asked Alana.

"Similar." Bethany nodded. "They're actually called buoyancy aids. Catch!" She threw one to each of us in turn and then showed us how to put them on.

"And finally," said Bethany, "your leash. It's the stringy thing attached to your board." It was a thin lead, kind of like a dog lead, but a bit stretchy. One end was attached to the board and the other end had a Velcro strap on it.

"I wondered what that was for," said Lyndz. She giggled. "I thought it might be in case your dog wanted to come surfing too!"

"The Velcro strap goes round your ankle," Bethany explained. "It means that if you let go of your board in the water, you won't lose it entirely. But, even so, *try* not to let go of your board. If a wave picks it up, it could hit you or another surfer, which wouldn't be fun."

So then we went into the water, right? Wrong. *Then* we all had to sit next to our boards while Bethany gave us a lecture about different sorts of winds and waves and stuff.

"When you get more advanced, you can paddle out to deeper water," said Bethany. "You should watch the waves – they normally come in a series, called a 'set'. Generally, there are three waves in a set, with a calm bit in between."

"I never knew that!" said Frankie, as if it was really interesting or something.

I pretended to swallow a yawn. "Are we going to get in the water any time this *year*, d'you reckon?" I whispered. I was starting to wish we were down with the others, playing beach volleyball.

But at *last* Bethany announced we could wade out and try some surfing for real.

The water was quite warm – thank goodness! But I didn't wade far. As soon as I saw a wave coming, I turned my board round. The wave caught me all right, but I didn't exactly shoot gracefully in to the beach – the wave flipped me straight over, and I ended up coughing and spluttering on the sand.

"Well done!" said Bethany. "At least you hung on to your board!"

On my next go I did manage to stay lying on my board. "Wheeeee!" I squealed as the wave raced in to the shore, taking me with it. This was more like it – this was *fun*!

Meanwhile, Bethany was standing in the shallow water shouting, "Go for it, Frankie!" and "That's right, Alana!" When she said, "Wow, Rosie – that's excellent!" I turned round and looked.

Coming in last of the group, Rosie had actually managed to kneel up on her board. Her mouth was wide open in astonishment – she looked like she was on a fairground ride.

"Brilliant!" Bethany said to her as she came out of the water. Rosie beamed.

"Well done!" squealed Lyndz. "You looked awesome!"

Even Miss Walsh – who was sitting on a towel further up the beach – gave her a round of applause.

That made me determined. I strode straight out into the waves again. I was so going to kneel up this time.

What actually happened was that I headed in to the beach bum first, with my board on top of me and a nose and mouth full of seawater.

"Don't worry, you'll get it soon too," grinned Bethany, wading over to where I was lying like a beached whale. "It's a knack – some people crack it quicker than others, that's all."

I didn't say anything then, but I can admit it to you now: I was a bit miffed at that. I mean, *I'm* the sporty member of the Sleepover Club, right? I know Lyndz does loads of horse-riding, but for your general, all-round, kick-about, get-the-knack sport girl, you'd come to me first every time, wouldn't you?

And yet here I was, clearly on a mission to drink a whole seaful of water, while Rosie was busy developing some serious skills.

I didn't have long to feel sorry for myself, though. Just as I was picking myself up, I heard a shriek. Out in the water, Fliss had fallen off her board and lost hold of it completely. Somehow, though, she'd managed to catch the wave just right and surf in lying on her tummy.

"That's called body surfing," Bethany called to her, laughing. "Fun, isn't it? Don't worry – your board didn't hit anyone. Just come out of the water and it'll follow."

Fliss must have been kneeling in the shallows – she was still submerged up to her neck.

"Come on, Fliss, come out!" called Frankie, who was sitting on the sand beside me.

"I – I can't!" said Fliss, looking panic-stricken. "I've lost my bikini bottoms! When the wave caught me they kind of swooshed off!"

Sure enough, a little way away, I could see something bright pink floating on the water. Frankie and I clutched each other, helpless with giggles.

"Just come out, don't worry," called Bethany.

"I'll wrap you in my towel!" called Miss Walsh.

Fliss looked mortified. Not only did she have Bethany, Miss Walsh, Alana and the rest of the Sleepover Club for an audience, but also, not far away, there was the other group, including Jude and Ryan Scott, any of whom might turn to look her way just at the wrong moment. I could hardly bear to imagine it – Fliss would *die* of embarrassment.

Somebody had to do something. Wiping my eyes with the back of my hand, I grabbed my board and yelled, "Don't worry, Fliss! Kenny to the rescue!" and charged into the water as fast as I could.

Thinking back, I realised it could have been dangerous. Fliss's pants could have bobbed away from me into seriously deep water. As Miss Walsh pointed out later, when she was ticking me off for being so rash, the pants might've caused a major incident, with the coastguard coming out and everything. Can you imagine *that*?

Luckily, though, after a couple of minutes

of paddling, I'd reached the pants. I grabbed them and set off back towards where Fliss was crouching.

"Thanks, Kenny," she spluttered, taking them from me and wriggling into them underwater. "I really, really owe you for this one!"

When we both got out of the water, we found that Rosie had managed to do her kneeling thing again, and was grinning away, pleased as anything. Alana, on the other hand, was sitting slumped on the sand with a piece of seaweed stuck in her hair, looking as miserable and bedraggled as one of Lyndz's cats when they've just been given a bath.

"Come on, Alana," Bethany was saying, patting her on the shoulder. "You were doing really well that last time. You've so nearly got it."

Alana shook her head. "It's too hard," she said. "I want to do volleyball." I think she'd swallowed even more water than me, so I did feel quite sorry for her.

"Bethany – can't you show us how it's *really*

done?" said Frankie. "I mean – it's a bit hard for us to imagine when we've never seen any proper surfing." The 'real surfers' down at the other end of the beach were too far away for us to see them except as blobs – with different coloured blobs for surfboards.

"Hey, yeah – please!" I said. "It'd be ace!"

Bethany didn't look at all keen. But I think being surrounded by five pleading faces – no, make that six: even Alana Banana looked interested – was more than she could resist. She heaved her shoulders up in a big sigh. "Well, I guess it might be an idea…"

"Yeeeeesssss!"

Unfortunately, our shouting had got the attention of Rude Jude (as Frankie called him) and the other group, and as Bethany strode out into the water, her board under her arm, the whole lot of them turned and stared.

"Don't look round, don't look round," I muttered to myself as I watched Bethany. I was pretty certain, having seen the tension earlier between her and Jude, that if Bethany knew she had an audience, she would go off the whole idea quicker than you could say "wipe out". (Which is the surfing term for falling off your board, by the way. Cool, huh?)

Luckily, Bethany didn't look round.

Lying flat on her board, she paddled out so that she could get a longer run in to the beach than we'd had. Then she turned and let a wave catch her board just perfectly. In one graceful movement, she stood up and came surfing straight in towards us. It was awesome.

We whooped and cheered as Bethany came out of the water. As we clustered round her, Lyndz nudged me and whispered, "Hey – check out Rude Jude." I turned. He was wading out into the water with his board under his arm.

"Copy cat," I said.

Lyndz nodded. "Bet he's going to do something really show-offy." She snorted. "Typical *boy*." And since Lyndz has four brothers, she should know!

Soon Bethany and the others saw that we were watching something and turned to look too. It would've been better if we'd all ignored Jude, of course, but I was *sooo* curious, and I bet the others felt the same. I was really hoping he'd fall in and make a complete fool of himself.

Jude paddled out much further than Bethany had. Then, at long last, just as a fairly big wave was building, he turned his board around.

What can I tell you? I have never seen anything like it. Jude didn't ride straight into the beach like Bethany. He went *along* the wall of this wave, down the face of it and up again, like a skateboarder in one of those concrete rinks.

When he had finished, there was a short silence. None of us knew what to say – we were all looking at Bethany.

"Well, I think we've done enough for one day," she said at last, smoothing her wet hair back from her face. "And anyway – don't you reckon it's about time for lunch?"

We all agreed with *that*.

5

"What *is* the trouble between Bethany and Jude?" said Rosie the next morning as we hurried to get dressed. It was our turn on breakfast duty, so we were supposed to be up earlier than anyone else.

"Did you notice that Rude Jude's group didn't even cheer him when he came out of the water yesterday?" said Frankie, pulling her t-shirt over her head. "He must've been really grumpy with them."

"He's a *loser*," said Lyndz fiercely. "He's horrible to Bethany and Bethany is just the coolest person ever!"

Frankie nodded. "If he shows off again today, we should all laugh at him."

"Uh! Ooooh!" puffed Fliss, trying to bend down to buckle her sandals. "Is anyone else *totally* stiff?"

"Me," I said.

"Me too," said Frankie, Lyndz and Rosie all at once.

"It's weird, because I know I'm not unfit," said Fliss, looking puzzled. "I go to aerobics *and* ballet."

Downstairs, we found Aidan already in the kitchen. "Morning, team!" he said, grinning at us. "Got a few aches and pains?" He must've been able to tell from our faces. "Don't worry about it," he laughed, handing out aprons. "You're just not accustomed to using your surfing muscles, that's all. The more you do it, the less it'll hurt."

78

"Great," whispered Fliss, not sounding at all convinced. "I think I'd rather sunbathe."

It turned out that the breakfast menu was already decided: porridge, with side servings of yoghurt, honey and chopped fruit.

Fliss groaned at the idea of porridge, but I didn't mind at all. We always have porridge when we go to see my gran and granddad in Glasgow and I really like it.

Aidan got Frankie, Lyndz and Fliss measuring out the milk and oats, and gave Rosie and me the fruit to chop. We had bananas, pears, apples and a few strawberries. Yum!

As he bent over the strawberries, picking out the bad ones, I noticed that Aidan's hair was wet. "You look like you've been down to the beach already!" I said.

I meant it as a joke – this early in the morning, I thought Aidan wouldn't have been further than the shower. But to my surprise he nodded. "That's right. Bethany's there now, as a matter of fact – you can often catch the best waves first thing. It's less crowded too."

"D'you reckon Bethany's a good surfer, Aidan?" said Frankie from the other side of the kitchen. "I mean – she looked really good to us yesterday, but we're not exactly experts."

"Oh, she's top," said Aidan, grinning.

"Is she as good as Jude?" asked Lyndz.

Immediately, I saw Aidan's smile fade. "Yes," he said firmly. "She's every bit as good as Jude – in my opinion, she's probably better. But there's no way Jude will admit that." He shook his head. "Jude Bailey is just one of those cavemen who can't bear the idea that a girl might beat him."

Yuck, I thought. What an idiot.

"I wish Bethany would surf for us properly," said Rosie.

Aidan smiled again. "Bethany's no show- off – unlike *some* people I could mention." Suddenly, he turned and looked round at us all. "Hey – if you really want to see how good she is, you should come down to the Surfing

Display Day on Saturday. You're still around then, right?"

We nodded. Saturday would be our last full day in Rawnston – we were due to head home on Sunday morning.

"Cool," said Aidan. "We want loads of support. The idea of the Display Day is to raise money for this anti-pollution charity called 'Surfers For Clean Water'. Believe me, there's nothing like surfing in skunky water to teach you how important it is to keep our beaches clean."

"What makes the water bad?" asked Lyndz. "Is it like when oil tankers leak and the birds all die? I've seen that on the telly."

"It's not just accidents like that," said Aidan. "Lots of waste gets pumped into the sea the whole time – industrial chemicals, sewage…"

Sewage, I thought. Like – human waste? Imagine surfing in that. Gross!

"Anyway, maybe we shouldn't talk about it while we're cooking – it'll put us all off breakfast," said Aidan, as he went to help the others light the gas on the cooker. "The *other* thing the Surfing Display Day is for is to improve our image with the locals round here. Lots of the older people think surfers are just scruffy layabouts. There's going to be a couple of surfing competitions – one for adults and one for kids – and then stuff on the beach like face-painting and food stalls."

"Sounds brilliant!" said Frankie.

"Are you going to enter the competition?" asked Fliss.

Aidan nodded. "Bethany too," he said. "And Jude. It might just be his day for getting beaten!"

By this time, we could hear chattering and laughter as our classmates thundered down the stairs and into the dining room. I reckoned everyone would be majorly hungry after all that sea air yesterday – and it was a good job, because we seemed to be making enough porridge to feed an army.

An hour later, we were on our way to the beach. "Urgh, talk about a heavy breakfast," said Lyndz, rubbing her stomach. "Put me in the sea today and I'm going to sink like a stone!"

"So, girls, how are you getting on with your surfing?" said a voice behind us. It was Mrs Weaver, wearing a big floppy sunhat and sunglasses. Isn't it dead weird seeing teachers in holiday gear? She said, "I hear from Miss Walsh that you had fun yesterday."

Yes, if you can call swallowing seawater fun, I thought.

"It was brilliant," said Rosie. "I want to do it all week!"

"Mrs Weaver, have you heard about the Surfing Display Day on Saturday?" I asked.

"No, Laura, what's that?"

I repeated what Aidan had told us, including the bit about raising money for the anti-pollution charity – I thought Mrs Weaver would approve of that.

"Can we go?" I said at last. "Please? It would be so good to see some expert surfers after we've had all these lessons."

"See how it's really done!" added Frankie enthusiastically.

Mrs Weaver pursed her lips. "Well… I'm afraid I couldn't let you five go on your own," she said. "It would have to be an activity for the entire group." She considered for a moment. Then she said, "Let me talk to Mrs Daniels and Miss Walsh, and find out more from Aidan and Bethany. We can see exactly what's involved and have a think about it – OK?"

When we got down to the beach, Bethany was already there. It was clear she'd been in the water. She was wearing a really cool wet-suit, with short sleeves and cut-off legs. She'd rolled the upper half of it down to her hips, so you could see the waterproof version of a crop top she was wearing underneath. I could tell from the look on Fliss's face that she was wondering where she could buy the entire outfit for herself.

"All right, guys," said Bethany, "let's carry on with what we were doing yesterday. Remember,

84

try to move smoothly from one position to another when you're on your board."

No problem. I was *very* good at moving smoothly from one position (lying on my board) to another (flailing around in the water). Somehow, though, I didn't think that was what Bethany had in mind.

Still, at least I was getting better at catching waves just at the right moment. And the second time I caught one, I nearly managed to kneel up. *Really* nearly.

"Did you see me, did you see me?" I spluttered to Bethany when I got to the beach.

"Good effort!" she nodded, giving me a thumbs-up. "Next time you'll do it!"

But the next time I had a go, Rosie completely upstaged me by standing up – that's right *standing up* – on her board. Only for a nanosecond, apparently (I missed it – too busy flailing), but hey, who's counting?

"Yeah!" she shouted, punching the air and jumping up and down at the edge of the water. "It's just *the* best feeling! You've *got* to do it, Kenny!"

I felt like tearing my hair out in frustration. When Bethany had given us her demonstration yesterday, she'd made standing on your board look like the easiest thing in the world. Today, "Keep practising" was all she could say to help. But what if I practised all week and never got the knack? What a miserable week of water swallowing that would be! Each time I fell in the water, I decided to throw in my surfing towel and go and join the volleyballers. And then each time I picked myself up and shook the seaweed out of my hair, I thought I'd give it just one more shot. Kenny's no quitter, right? And besides, the next time might be the time I cracked it.

By lunchtime, everyone had knelt on their board at least once – everyone, that is, except me. It was really starting to get me down.

Today we'd all been given packed lunches in brown paper bags. Mrs Weaver insisted we find some shade to sit in while we ate – "I don't want anyone getting sunstroke!" she kept saying – so most of the surfers went with Miss Walsh to a picnic area behind a row of beach huts.

"Hey – over here, guys," I said, beckoning the rest of the Sleepover Club to a scrubby patch of sandy grass away from the others. I wanted to take my mind off my surfing disaster, and I had a great idea for how to do it.

"Listen," I said, "when are we having our midnight feast? How about tonight?"

"Yes – while the weather's good," said Fliss. "You never know when it might turn cold and rainy." The others nodded.

"Is there anything in here we can save for it?" said Lyndz, peering into her lunch bag.

"I've got some chocolate back at the hostel," said Rosie. "I hope it hasn't melted."

"How about these?" said Frankie, pulling a little packet of biscuits out of her lunch bag.

"Where's it going to be, then?" asked Lyndz, looking round at the rest of us.

87

"On the beach – definitely," I said. "Just imagine it – sitting under the stars, listening to the waves..."

"Eating chocolate biscuits," put in Lyndz.

"Eating chocolate biscuits," I nodded. "Come on, guys – wouldn't it be the most amazing thing ever?"

"The beach in the moonlight – it'd be *so* romantic!" said Fliss.

"I'm not sure, Kenny," said Rosie. "We'd get into major trouble if someone found out. Didn't you hear what Mrs Daniels said yesterday? Anyone caught misbehaving has to spend the rest of the week at the hostel, cleaning the kitchen and bathrooms."

"No one'll find out," I said breezily. "Just don't talk about it in front of other people – especially nosy types with flappy ears, like the M&Ms." I was pretty proud of myself – I'd ignored them totally so far this holiday.

Rosie still didn't look too sure. But then, she

was getting a major kick out of her surfing success – I needed something else to cheer me up. And a midnight adventure sounded like just the thing.

No *way* did I suspect, though, just how adventurous it was going to be.

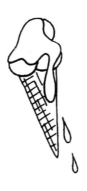

6

Running as hard as I could, my feet slipping and sludging into the sand, I made it past fourth base.

"Home run! Yeeeaaaahhhh!"

It was the afternoon and our whole class was playing a game of rounders, which was a real laugh. Aidan and Bethany had the afternoon off, so they'd both headed down to the serious surfers' end of the beach. Rosie was dying to go and watch them, but Mrs Weaver said no.

The rounders had really perked me up. I'd hit some great shots and made some seriously cool catches too, so by the time we packed up our stuff and headed back to the hostel I'd practically forgotten how bad I was at surfing.

And the best of it was, there was still our midnight feast to look forward to!

But when we got to the hostel, and everyone piled into their bedrooms to strip off their beach gear, I discovered that it wasn't just Rosie who had the collywobbles about our beach-trip plans.

"It'll be scary, Kenny," said Fliss, who was sitting on her bed, wriggling out of one set of clothes and into another. "It'll be really dark..."

"What about the romantic moonlight you were so keen on?"

"There might not *be* any moonlight," she said. "And then we'll just have our torches, and what if there are, you know, muggers and murderers around?"

"They might pick us off one by one," said

Rosie, her eyes wide with fright. "I'll keep sweeping my torch beam round the group, and each time it goes round there'll be one person less. Someone else missing…"

"Don't be ridiculous!" I snorted. "It might be a bit *spooky*, sure – but that'll be fun! Won't it?" Even though it was a blazing hot afternoon, Fliss shivered. I looked at the others.

Lyndz shrugged uncertainly. "Well… what if a high tide comes in really quickly? We could get swept out to sea."

"What is it with you lot?" I said crossly, flinging down my damp swimming costume. "It's all doom and gloom and the end of the world!" Though I couldn't admit it, I knew they had a point. Going all the way to the beach in the middle of the night would be more daring than anything we'd ever done before.

I tried to swallow my disappointment. "OK, OK," I said. "So what's it going to be instead? I guess we'll just have to stay in our bedroom, like when we have sleepovers at home."

"Not necessarily," said Frankie. She scrambled down the ladder of her bunk bed and headed for the window. "What about the garden here?" She leant over the sill for a moment, inspecting the view, and then turned back to face us. "I mean – we'll still get the moonlight, if there is any, and the stars and all that. It'll be dead quiet, so maybe we'll even be able to hear the sea in the distance. It could be fun."

"Genius idea!" said Lyndz.

I went to the window and squashed up next to Frankie to have a look. The garden was big, with lots of trees. It would be quite easy, I thought, to find a spot where we couldn't be seen from the house. "And we'll still have to think of a way to sneak out of the building," I said. That was one of the bits I was looking forward to the most. I nodded. "Yep. I reckon it'll be cool."

"Sounds good to me," agreed Fliss.

"Someone could hide in the bushes in the garden," said Rosie. "And they could drag us off one by one…"

"*Rosie!!!!*" the rest of us shouted together.

She snapped to attention, as if she'd been daydreaming. "Sorry, guys. I think I've been watching too much rubbishy TV."

The tricky bit was staying awake after lights-out, waiting long enough for everyone else to have gone to sleep. All the surfing and running about we'd done today had left us pretty exhausted.

"Couldn't we just have a little nap first?" said Lyndz as we all lay waiting in the dark. She yawned. "I could set my alarm clock…"

"I'll feel groggy if we do that," said Fliss. "I won't want to get up if I've been to sleep."

"I… didn't say you… had to snooze," said Lyndz, sounding snoozy. "Just me…"

"No one is going to sleep!" I laughed, flicking on my torch and shining it down into the bunk below Frankie, straight into Lyndz's face.

"Hey!" she grumbled, shading her eyes.

At last, when the luminous hands on my watch said a quarter to midnight, I thought we were pretty safe. We rolled out of bed, pulled sweatshirts and jeans on over our pyjamas, and stuffed our feet into our trainers. Then, opening the door really slowly so that it wouldn't squeak, we crept out on to the landing.

"Torches off," I whispered. "Don't take any chances."

There was just enough of a dim glow slanting through the landing window for us to make it down the stairs without falling over each other.

"Which window are we heading for again?" hissed Lyndz behind me.

"The little one in the kitchen," I whispered.

Downstairs, we crossed the hallway and made it as far as the kitchen door. It was shut.

"This is creepy," breathed Rosie. "Someone might be in there."

"Shhh!" said Frankie.

I put my hand on the doorknob and turned

it slowly. As the door opened, I clicked on my torch – I didn't dare switch on the main light.

"OK, I'll go first," I whispered.

The kitchen window was fairly small and hinged at the side. I turned the handle on the latch and pushed it open. Then I sat on the sill and folded first one leg through, then the other. Jumping down into the flowerbed, I turned and whispered, "Easy!"

Lyndz was next. She got one leg through and then stopped. Her head was wedged at a funny angle. I could see she was trying to get the other leg up to the sill, but somehow there wasn't room.

"Oh help – I'm stuck!" she whispered.

You know that bit in Winnie the Pooh when he gets stuck in the rabbit hole and has to stay there for days? I was worried that that was how it was going to be with Lyndz. I could just imagine the teachers coming down to breakfast in the morning and finding her wedged in the kitchen window.

 96

"Push her from behind!" I hissed to the others.

"Ouch!" squealed Lyndz.

"Shhh!"

In the end, I had to push Lyndz backwards into the kitchen again. She came through the next time head first and landed in a heap in the flowerbed.

"Oh no! I think I've crushed the biscuits!" she said, dusting herself down.

A minute later, the whole gang had made it through. Frankie carefully left the window ajar, so that we'd be able to get back the same way, and we set off, creeping across the lawn to find a good feasting place.

We needed a spot that was hidden from the house, so that we wouldn't be the first thing anyone spied if they happened to look out of their bedroom window.

"Behind those trees?" hissed Rosie, nodding towards the far end of the garden nearest the road.

Frankie shook her head. "I checked it out

earlier," she said. "The space between the trees and the fence is really narrow. It's got lots of old crisp packets, too, that people walking by have chucked over."

"Yuck," said Fliss.

"What about there?" I whispered, shining my torch beam towards a clump of bushes over on our right. "Is there any grass on the other side?"

Frankie shrugged.

"Wait here, team, I'll go and investigate," I said. Trying to be light on my feet, I ran across to the bushes. Behind them there was a flat and comfy-looking patch of grass – perfect! I held my torch under my chin, so that it lit up my face, and grinned and nodded at the others. They came scampering over.

I reckon it was one of the best midnight feasts the Sleepover Club has ever had. We sat down on the grass in a circle, put our torches in the middle, and got down to munching crushed biscuits (Lyndz's), half-melted chocolate (Rosie's), plus a whole pile of sherbet sweets, liquorice laces and jelly babies that Frankie, Fliss and I had brought from home.

"You can hear the sea – listen!" whispered Frankie.

"And look at all these stars," said Rosie, flopping on to her back. "There are loads more here than in Cuddington."

"There can't *be* more," I said, lying down too. "It must just be that there aren't so many street lights, so you can *see* more."

Then we talked about Aidan, Bethany and Jude, and had a complete giggling fit about all the rude things we'd say to Rude Jude if we got the chance.

"I'd tell him he's a ssssnotty sssaddo!" spluttered Rosie, spraying out biscuit crumbs with every "s".

"With rancid custard for brains!" added Lyndz.

"I'd tell him he should hang out with the M&Ms," said Fliss. "He's just about their level."

99

"Rude Jude, Crude Jude, Booed Jude, Moody Jude…" said Frankie.

"Pooed Jude!" I put in. Lyndz, who'd just taken a great big swig of orangeade, burst out laughing and sprayed the orangeade all over Rosie. Rosie shrieked.

"Hey, not so loud!" hissed Frankie urgently, clamping her finger to her lips. Instantly, we all turned ultra-serious, holding our breath and looking towards the house. I was convinced we were going to see a light switch on at any moment.

Ten seconds passed.

Then twenty.

Nothing happened.

"Phew, that was close," said Lyndz, relaxing again. "Sorry, Rosie."

"It's OK," said Rosie. Lyndz pulled off her sweatshirt and wiped the worst of the orangeade out of Rosie's hair.

"I hope we get to go shopping this week," said Fliss when we'd calmed down a bit. "I want to find out where Bethany gets her clothes."

A few minutes later Frankie said, "Hey – let's take it in turns to tell ghost stories!"

"No," said Rosie firmly. "Unless you want me to start *really* screaming."

Fliss knelt up and put her hands on her bottom. "I thought so," she said. "This grass is damp. And is anyone else cold or is it just me?"

"I'm freezing, actually," admitted Lyndz.

"Maybe it's time to go back," said Frankie.

"Make sure we've got every scrap of rubbish," I said as we began tidying up. "We mustn't leave any evidence."

At last, with all our bits and pieces stuffed back into our bags, and with our torches in our hands, we set off again across the garden, Rosie leading the way. Suddenly, my stomach lurched with worry: what if someone woke up and caught us at the last minute – when we were so nearly home and dry? It would be just our luck. By now, Rosie was standing in the flowerbed, fumbling with the window.

"Come on!" I whispered urgently. "Hurry up!"

"But – but I can't," stammered Rosie.

"Don't be silly – you managed on the way out. Just sit on the sill…"

"No, it's not that," said Rosie. "It's the window. It's shut."

7

"*What?*"

"It can't be!"

"Are you sure it's the right window?"

"Yes! Look!"

I pushed ahead of Rosie and looked for myself.

"What are we going to do?" said Fliss.

"It's spooky," whispered Lyndz. "It's as if someone's been watching us. They saw us come out here and now they've shut the window so we can't get back."

103

"Don't be silly," hissed Frankie. "If anyone knew we were here, they'd come and tell us off, wouldn't they? Either that or rat on us." She shook her head. "One of the teachers probably got up to go to the loo or get a drink of water or something, noticed the window was open and shut it. That's all."

"Well, never mind *who* shut it, it's shut – that's the problem," I said. "So how are we going to get back in?"

"We won't have to spend all night out here, will we?" said Fliss, her teeth beginning to chatter. "We'll freeze."

"There's nothing else for it – we'll have to break the glass," said Lyndz.

"What – wake everyone up and make them think they're being burgled?" I said. "Just think how much trouble we'd get into! They'd probably call the police."

"Maybe we could throw bits of gravel at someone's bedroom window," suggested Rosie. "Just enough to wake them up. Someone who'd help us without telling the teachers."

There was silence for a minute as we all tried to remember who was sleeping in which bedroom. Frankie groaned. "Imagine if we woke the M&Ms up by mistake. They'd just *love* landing us right in it!"

All of a sudden we heard a noise.

"What's that?" gasped Lyndz, clutching my sleeve.

"Sounds like a car," said Frankie.

"It *is* a car," I hissed. "And it's coming up the drive. Quick – get behind this bush. *Now!*"

We crouched together behind the bush, huddled as close as if we were playing Sardines. "Oh no, this is a disaster," whispered Fliss shakily. "We're bound to get caught."

"Who would come to the house at this time of night?" whispered Rosie. "You don't think it's a real burglar, do you?"

There was no way around it – you had to admit it was a weird time to be visiting. So far the car had been half-hidden by the trees that lined the drive – now it came into full view, as it swung round in front of the house. I bobbed my head up, so I could see over the bush.

"It's got a surfboard strapped to the roof," I hissed to the others.

"A surfing burglar, then." Fliss shuddered.

"It looks like an old car – pretty battered," whispered Frankie, who'd bobbed up beside me.

The car's engine stopped and the headlights flicked off. Then the driver got out. At first, I couldn't make out anything except a vague shape – but the next minute the moon emerged from behind a cloud and a dim silvery light flooded the driveway. It revealed a familiar tall figure creeping over the gravel towards the house, evidently trying not to make any noise.

"It's Aidan!" Frankie and I whispered together. Rosie, Lyndz and Fliss peered round the bush. Fliss sighed with relief.

"Do you think we could dash in through the door when he's not looking?" said Rosie.

106

"How would he miss all five of us?" said Lyndz. "He'd have to close his eyes and count to twenty!"

"One of us could sneak in and hide till he's gone to bed, then open the window," Frankie suggested.

"He's unlocking the door," I said. "If we don't do something right now, we're going to miss our chance." And without giving myself time to think, I raced out from behind the bush.

It was a mad plan. In order to reach the door before Aidan shut it behind him, I had to run as fast as my legs would carry me – there was no time for dodging from shadow to shadow.

Of course, Aidan saw me. For a split second, he looked seriously startled – then he recognised me and frowned. "What on earth are you doing?" he whispered as I reached him.

"We were having a midnight feast in the garden," I panted. "Someone shut the window so we can't get back in."

Aidan put a finger to his lips. He didn't want

to hear any more. I turned and beckoned to the others. Sheepishly, they climbed out from behind the bush and made their way towards us.

"Quietly," Aidan mouthed as we tiptoed past him into the hall.

I half expected that he might want to wake the teachers straight away, but he flapped an arm in the direction of the stairs, meaning we should go up to bed.

We crept into our room and flopped on to our bunks.

"We're really for it now," whispered Lyndz. "He's bound to tell Weaver in the morning."

"But Aidan's nice!" protested Fliss.

"However nice he is, it's his job," said Lyndz grimly.

"Do you think we'll be grounded?" whispered Rosie.

"Cleaning, all day every day for the rest of the week – ugh," groaned Frankie. "And I bet they'll make us miss the Display Day too."

I didn't sleep very well – and I don't think the others did either. In the morning, the mood in our room was a real downer. "When d'you think we'll get the summons from Weaver?" asked Lyndz, leaning up on one elbow and rubbing her eyes. "Before breakfast or after?"

No one knew. As we got dressed, we expected a knock on our door at every moment. But we made it down to breakfast without anything happening. In the dining room we eyed the teachers anxiously as we crunched our cornflakes, but from what we could see they weren't in a bad mood, and they didn't seem to be talking about us either.

We'd signed up for surfing again, of course, and after breakfast we strolled down to the beach.

"Maybe Weaver's decided to let us off," said Rosie, squirting sunscreen spray on to her arms as she walked along.

Frankie snorted. "When has Weaver let anyone off anything? No – there's only one answer: Aidan hasn't told her."

"See, I *said* he was nice!" said Fliss triumphantly. "Hey, Rosie – will you spray some of that on me?"

I thought it over as we walked along. To be honest, though I knew Aidan was nice, I was surprised he was *that* nice. He hadn't looked at all pleased when he'd first caught sight of me dashing towards him like a mad garden ghost last night.

Lyndz was walking next to me. Noticing my puzzled expression, she shrugged. "One thing's for sure," she said, hitching her beach bag higher on her shoulder, "we owe him – big time."

That day we had a wicked time on the beach. I don't know what it was – the lack of sleep? The hours spent lying awake thinking about getting grounded? – but something had happened to my surfing skills overnight. Maybe, with everything else that'd been going on, I just wasn't worrying about it any more. At any rate today, suddenly, everything felt a whole heap easier.

"Go, Kenny!" yelled Bethany as, on my very first attempt, I knelt up smoothly on my board.

I screamed and whooped and shrieked. The feeling of the sea beneath me – the power of the wave pushing me along – was MEGA amazing. It felt like the best funfair ride ever.

And then, about one hour and a trillion wipe-outs later, a miracle happened: the wave caught my board, I pushed up on my arms, and my feet slipped under me really easily to a crouching position. A moment after that, I stood up. I was surfing – really surfing!

Of course, the very next second I toppled over and fell in with an almighty KER-SPLOSH! But nothing could wipe the grin off my face when I resurfaced.

"You were *awesome*!" squealed Frankie, splashing up and down in the shallows. "Way to go, wave warrior!"

I reckon all five members of the Sleepover Club turned into wave warriors that afternoon. We still fell in loads, of course, but now we were having serious fun. "I'm so proud of you guys!" said Bethany when, lesson over, we flopped on to the sand to dry off.

"We're proud of us too!" I said and everyone laughed.

That evening, the Sleepover Club made up part of the group whose turn it was to cook dinner, along with Alana Banana, Simon Baxter and Danny McCloud. Aidan and Bethany were helping out, of course, and – as we chopped vegetables and opened tins of tomatoes (we were making vegetable lasagne) – Bethany told Aidan all about the ace progress we'd made with our surfing.

"Seriously well done," said Aidan, grinning and nodding at us. "Getting started at surfing takes hard work."

"He's obviously not narked with us, anyway," whispered Frankie to me as she handed me the olive oil.

A little later, when Alana, Simon and Danny were busy around the oven on the other side of the room, I sidled up to Aidan and said in a low voice, "By the way, we just wanted to say thanks – for not telling the teachers about last night."

"Well, I wanted to say exactly the same thing to you lot," replied Aidan, equally quietly.

"What for?"

"I wasn't supposed to be creeping around in the dark either," he said. "You could've got me into serious trouble if you'd told anyone."

"What were you doing, then?" asked Rosie, who'd been listening in. "You're not really a burglar, are you?"

Aidan laughed. "No! I got a text message late last night from one of my mates. He'd seen on the surfcam – that's a webcam we've set up at the beach – that there were some really good waves." Aidan looked over his shoulder, checking that Bethany couldn't hear – but she'd gone down to the cellar for some more bottles of water. "So," he said, "a group of us went and surfed in the moonlight. It was *excellent*."

"But isn't it dangerous, surfing at night?" I asked.

Aidan grimaced. "To be honest, it is – although at least I was with friends. It's definitely something I'd never do alone." He looked round at us – the whole Sleepover Club was listening to him now. "That's partly why I'm glad you didn't say anything – I wasn't exactly setting a good example, was I? The other thing is, I'm supposed to have a curfew while I'm working here – no late nights on the town for me!"

At that moment, Bethany came back in with an armful of plastic bottles. "What's that, Ade?"

"Hmm?" Aidan pretended suddenly to be very interested in the courgette he was chopping. "Oh, nothing," he said. But when Bethany turned her back again, he looked at Frankie and me and gave us a friendly wink.

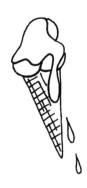

8

Our vegetable lasagne went down a storm. I've never been that interested in cooking, to tell you the truth, but it actually felt really cool to see everyone munching away happily and passing their plates along for seconds.

"I'm amazed – it was dead easy to make," said Frankie, reaching for another piece of garlic bread. Like me, her cooking skills don't usually go much further than a peanut butter sandwich.

"Sssh! Don't let on!" hissed Lyndz. "Tell everyone

it was really tricky and we're all going to be the next Jamie Oliver!"

"Lovely jubbly," said Fliss, doing the worst impression of Jamie Oliver I've ever seen. Frankie and I nearly fell off the bench laughing.

Just then, Mrs Weaver clapped her hands. "Settle down a moment, everyone!" Frankie was still clutching me and quaking. I sniffed hard and wiped my eyes with my sleeve.

"I just wanted to announce," said Mrs Weaver, "that there's been a change of plan for the end of the week."

"We're not going home!" Danny McCloud shouted out. Everyone laughed and then cheered.

Mrs Weaver smiled. She was miles more relaxed than usual – back at school she would've told Danny off for interrupting. Now she just flapped her hands to make everyone quieten down again and then said, "I'm afraid not, Danny. But I'm glad you're all enjoying yourselves so much. I think we should say a big thank you to Bethany and Aidan for that..."

We didn't need any encouragement – instantly, whoops and cheers and whistles broke out all around the room. Bethany and Aidan stood up, grinning, and bowed to one side of the room and then the other. I reckon the Sleepover Club made more noise than anyone, we were still so grateful to Aidan for not getting us into trouble!

When Aidan and Bethany had sat down again, Mrs Weaver went on, "What I want to announce is that on Saturday we'll all be attending the Surfing Display Day down at the beach…"

And while she explained to everyone what it was, the five of us – who knew already, of course – looked round at each other.

"Excellent!" said Frankie.

I did a Tim Henman clenched fist. "Re*sult!*"

"Bethany's going to win the surfing competition," whispered Rosie. "And Jude's going to get a *rude* awakening!"

When Mrs Weaver had finished explaining about the Display Day, she said, "Just one more thing…" We all turned to listen. "Tomorrow evening, with Aidan and Bethany's kind assistance, we're going to hold a special event of our own: a barbecue on the beach."

There was a second of silence. Then the whole class erupted. The cheering for Aidan and Bethany a minute ago had been nothing compared to *this*. You could have heard us down at the beach, I reckon!

"Everything's going so well," sighed Rosie after supper. We were sitting in the garden – since we'd cooked, we were excused washing-up duties. Rosie lay back, folding her arms behind her head. "Aidan covered for us, we're getting to go to the Display Day, like we wanted – and now there's the barbecue too. I think I must've died and gone to heaven!"

"It's almost strange," said Fliss, pushing her sunglasses up on to her forehead. "A whole week away and nothing's gone wrong – it's got to be a record. No teacher trouble, no hassle from the M&Ms – perfect!"

Now, I'm not usually superstitious – black cats can cross my path whenever they like (and I can't even remember whether that's supposed to be good luck or bad) – but right then something made me say, "Hey, be careful – famous last words! Hadn't someone better touch wood?"

No one could be bothered to get up and run across to the nearest tree – not even me. But Lyndz, who was sitting next to me, looked at me in surprise. "C'mon Kenny – relax," she said. "What could possibly go wrong now?"

I pulled at a few tufts of grass and then tossed them in the air, watching as they floated away on the breeze. "Sorry," I said. "I'm being silly." Nothing could go wrong – not now. Could it?

The next morning, our routine changed – we didn't go down to the beach. Instead, everyone had to stay at the hostel and help clean the bathrooms, the kitchen and the dining hall – which was a bit of a downer, I must admit. "What did they say this was supposed to do – help build our team spirit or something?" said Frankie as she scrubbed one of the basins.

"Couldn't we just've had another game of rounders?" said Fliss, who was leaning so far into the bath she was cleaning, she looked like she was about to fall in.

The one good thing was that, with the whole class on the case, "Operation Mop" didn't take long. By lunchtime, we were done and, as we all sat in the dining hall eating the sandwiches Bethany and Aidan had made for us, Mrs Daniels told us what the afternoon held in store.

"We've got the barbecue to look forward to this evening, of course," she said – as if any of us would have forgotten! "But between now and then we'd like you to split up into groups and explore Rawnston a little. There are lots of interesting things to see: a fine Norman church, the local museum, the library…"

"Sounds *thrilling*," Frankie mumbled into her sandwich.

"No, it'll be great," whispered Fliss excitedly. "We can go shopping!"

"It's very important that you stay in groups of at *least* three," Mrs Daniels went on. "And no one is allowed to spend the afternoon on the beach – it's far too dangerous when you are unsupervised. It is absolutely forbidden, understood?"

"Yes, Mrs Daniels," we chorused.

"Good. Miss Walsh will now come round and hand out maps of Rawnston, as well as a little questionnaire I've devised, which I hope you'll find enjoyable. If you answer the questions in order, they take you on a route round the town…"

"What's the questionnaire like?" asked Lyndz after Miss Walsh had visited our table.

I found the right page and scanned down a few questions.

"How many gargoyles can you find on the outside of Rawnston church?" I read out. "What's the oldest exhibit in Rawnston museum?" Next to each question there was a dotted line on which you were supposed to write the answer.

"Could be quite fun, I guess," said Rosie.

"It's a bit like a treasure hunt," said Frankie. "Except without the treasure."

Naturally, Fliss had to get changed before we set off. After what felt like about three hours' umming and ahhing, she picked out a blue and white dress and blue flip-flops with sequins on. I reckon she wanted to impress the people in all the cool cafés and shops we'd seen from the coach when we first drove into Rawnston. She certainly didn't seem that interested in Mrs Daniels' questionnaire.

Rosie had taken charge of it. As we walked into the town centre, she squinted at the paper in the bright sunshine. "We're supposed to start at the war memorial in the middle of Market Square."

Fliss had other ideas. "Hey, check out this shop!" she said suddenly, grabbing Rosie's elbow and dragging her down a side street. The rest of us followed.

It was a surfing shop. In the window there were loads of boards of different sizes, decorated with crazy squiggly writing and designs showing waves or stars or silhouettes of surfers. There were lots of clothes and accessories in the window too – baggy shorts, thick-soled flip-flops, different kinds of wetsuits, leashes and big patches to stick on your board to help you grip.

"Can we go in?" said Fliss. Though most of the clothes in the shop seemed to be for boys, she'd spotted a rack of stretchy dresses just inside the door.

"No..." Rosie murmured, trying to back away. "The sales assistants look scary."

I could see what she meant. A boy and a girl who both looked about eighteen were leaning against the shop counter, staring at us. They had identical blond, tangly hair and were both really tanned – you could tell they were surfers. They were wearing the same kind of clothes as Bethany and Aidan, but they didn't look half so friendly.

"They just fancy themselves, that's all," I said. I recognised the look on their faces from my older sisters, Emma and Molly. They put on exactly the same sneery expression sometimes when they're looking at me. Thing is, I know they're not cool or trendy – they just think they are – so I tend to yell "Bumface!" at them and run away.

I wasn't sure that was the best thing to do right now, however. And once Fliss had dragged her eyes away from the clothes and taken a proper look at the assistants, she didn't seem so keen on going in, either. "Let's see what other shops there are," she muttered. "It looks expensive in there."

It turned out that there were loads of other surfing shops – Rawnston was crawling with them. As soon as we spotted one where the assistants didn't look like they wanted to eat us for lunch, we dived in.

"Wow – look at these dresses!" Frankie had found a rack of brightly coloured clingy things with spaghetti straps.

"They are *so* cool!" said Rosie.

"I like the hot pants," said Fliss, holding a pair against her hips. "What do you think?"

Rosie sighed. "My mum would kill me if I bought anything like that."

"Hmm." Fliss looked down at the hot pants, then turned to face the mirror. "Mine too, probably. Spoilsport!"

Fliss put the hot pants back and bought a funky plastic ring and a load of jangly bangles instead. By this time we were hot and thirsty. Frankie spotted a café called Crush on the other side of the square.

The café looked majorly cool, but even I had to admit it was pretty intimidating. Loads of teenagers were sprawled around the tables outside, chatting and laughing and watching everyone who walked past.

"Uh – why don't we follow the questionnaire

125

for a bit?" suggested Lyndz. "I guess we ought to fill in a few answers, just in case Mrs Daniels wants to check where we've been."

"Good thinking," said Frankie. "But first I'm going in there for a can of Coke." She pointed to the café. "Who's coming?"

There was a moment's silence. Then, "Me," I said firmly. No Rawnston versions of Emma and Molly were going to get the better of me! I straightened my Leicester City t-shirt, put my shoulders back and my nose in the air. Then Frankie and I marched into the café.

It's a funny thing, when people try to make you feel small – have you noticed that it doesn't work unless *you agree to it*? After all, who could make you feel bad just by looking at you? That would be a pretty major magic trick. No – for it to work, you have to join in. So all you have to do to *stop* it working is *not* join in, right?

Right. But it's certainly easier said than done.

As Frankie and I walked side by side past all those lolling trendy types, I could feel their eyes swivelling to follow us. Frankie was pretending we were having a conversation. "I fancy a Coke," she said loudly – even though I knew that already. "What do you want, Kenny?"

"Er… uh…" I was concentrating on putting one foot in front of the other. I didn't have much spare brain left for speaking.

But in fact, once we got inside the café, things were loads better. There weren't so many people, for a start – the customers were all catching the rays outside – and the woman behind the counter looked a bit like Rosie's mum, which made me relax straight away.

"A can of Coke to go please," said Frankie.

Two minutes later we'd rejoined the others on the far side of the square and I felt like I'd just climbed Mount Everest.

"Lead on, keeper of the questionnaire!" Frankie said to Rosie, taking a slurp from her can. "Where first?"

We looked at the war memorial and spent a while in the town museum – which had some

127

excellent photographs of old Rawnston football teams in funny shorts. Then we headed for the church to count the gargoyles.

"I make it thirteen," said Lyndz, after she'd stumbled right round the building.

"Fourteen! Definitely fourteen!" said Fliss, who'd been round the other way.

Inside the church it was shadowy and cool, which was a relief after the heat outside. We spent a while reading the wall plaques and the tombs and looking at the stained glass windows.

"Excellent – they've got a Visitors' Book!" said Lyndz. "We should all sign. And then we can come back in twenty years when we're really crumbly and look at our signatures."

"Brilliant idea!" said Frankie. "Let's do it!"

We each signed our name in our best handwriting and wrote Cuddington Primary in the Address column. Rosie was the last to sign. "Rosie... Maria... Cartwright," she muttered as she bent over the book.

"There we are – it's down on record," she said a minute later, clicking the top back on to the pen.

"What've you put?" Lyndz asked, craning to see over her shoulder. Then she squealed, "Rosie! You're outrageous!"

That brought the rest of us hurrying as fast as we thought you were allowed to in a church. "What? What?" said Fliss breathlessly.

"Look!" Lyndz held up the Visitors' Book. Under Occupation – a column the rest of us had left blank – Rosie had written:

Wave Wavvior

"I wonder what we'll write there when we come back in twenty years," said Fliss. But before she could start telling us about her plans to become a model – *again* – Frankie said, "Hey – you know what I really fancy doing?"

"What's that?" I said.

"I fancy checking out that end of the beach

where the real surfers go. See if Bethany and Aidan are there."

"And Jude," said Rosie.

"But we're not allowed on the beach," began Fliss. "Remember what Mrs Weaver said…"

"I know, I know," Frankie cut in. "But next to the sand, isn't there a grassy area with a pathway?"

"There was by our bit," I nodded, thinking about the place where we had our surfing lessons. "The path runs behind the beach huts."

"And it probably carries on right along the whole length of the beach," said Frankie.

"We could go and see if it does, anyway," said Rosie eagerly. "And it's not *part* of the beach, so we wouldn't be breaking any rules."

"Exactly," said Frankie. She laughed. "Don't look so worried, Fliss! Weaver'll never find out in any case. Come on, let's go."

Frankie's hunch was right. The path did stretch right along the edge of the beach, tracking through the grassy area that was the last bit before the sand started. As we followed the path past where we'd had our lessons, it began to climb a little – the grassy bank rose higher than the sand, and every so often we saw sets of rough steps that people had made in the rocks, leading down to the beach.

This meant that by the time we got to the place the serious surfers used, the path was high enough up to give us a really good view of the water. There were quite a few people out there. We sat down to watch.

"They are *really* good," said Rosie after a minute. "Doesn't it look great when they turn quickly and the water swooshes up?"

"They do look cool," Fliss admitted. "They make it look really easy too. They must practise *all* the time."

"That's Jude," said Lyndz, shading her eyes.

"No, no – *that's* Jude." Frankie pointed. "The one with his wetsuit rolled down."

"Oh, yes. And there's Bethany!" Lyndz

exclaimed. "Look – just going into the water, with the red surfboard."

"I see her! Cool!" Rosie knelt up excitedly.

We all watched Bethany as she lay on her board and paddled out. Then she sat up, waiting as a set of waves approached. At the last minute, she turned her board around. The first wave caught her and she stood up, heading across the wave, parallel to the beach.

Suddenly, we saw Jude not far from Bethany, just about to stand up on his board.

"Hey – what's he doing?" I said. "That's her wave!"

"He's not going to drop in on her, is he?" said Frankie.

Bethany had explained 'dropping in' to us in our last surfing lesson. It's when one person cuts in front of another on the same wave. It's really rude, for a start – but it's really dangerous too, because it might cause a crash.

It seemed as if Rude Jude was living up to his name.

"But it's Bethany's wave!" protested Rosie, clenching her fists in frustration. "She got there first!"

We all knew it and we were certain Jude knew it too. But there was nothing any of us could do.

As we watched, Bethany caught sight of Jude and pushed on her board with her back foot, desperately trying to slow herself down. But it wasn't enough. Jude was right in her path, and though she tried to angle herself in towards the beach to avoid him, it was too late.

A moment later, in a great spray of water, they crashed.

For one heart-stopping moment, as the water bubbled and frothed, Bethany and Jude totally disappeared. Then Jude's head resurfaced – and Bethany's followed.

"They're moving about," breathed Frankie beside me. "They must be OK." At the moment of the crash, without thinking, we'd grabbed one another's hands. Now we held on, our eyes fixed on the distant water.

It looked as if Bethany and Jude were

heading for the beach. As the wave had broken over them, it had swept them part of theway in, so at least they didn't have far to go.

"Jude's trying to help her out of the water," said Rosie.

"And she's pushing him away," I said. "Look!"

Even from this distance, Bethany looked pretty angry. Once she was in shallow enough water to be able to stand, she started wading painfully slowly towards the beach. Jude tried to take her arm and put it around his shoulders so that he could support her, but she shrugged him off.

"She must be hurt," said Rosie. Then she gasped. "Ohmigosh!"

There was blood – lots of it – running down Bethany's right leg.

I scrambled to my feet. "We have to go and help!"

"We can't... we're not allowed on the beach."

"Fliss, this is an emergency!" I said. "Bethany's

135

hurt – who cares about rules? Come on!"

I dashed to the nearest set of steps and half-climbed, half-slithered down them on to the sand. Then I set off running, with the others following close behind.

As I got nearer to Bethany, I saw her sit down on the sand, grimacing with pain, so that she could untie the leash from her ankle. Jude bent over her, but I heard her snap, "Leave me alone, you jerk! You've done enough damage already!" Jude straightened up and walked away.

A huddle of his friends soon closed round him. I heard one of them say, "Hey, mate, is your board all right? Any damage?" And another added, "Girls are rubbish surfers – why can't they stay out of our way?"

Jude didn't reply, but I wanted to shout, "Are you blind? It was *his* fault!" But I didn't have enough breath to waste on them. I reached Bethany and skidded down on to my knees in front of her.

"Hey – you OK?"

It was a silly question. The gash, which was on her shin, looked pretty nasty and there was a lot of blood. As the others caught up, I could see Fliss and Lyndz starting to look queasy. They don't have much stomach for gore. I'm lucky that it doesn't faze me – especially since I want to be a doctor. No use being a surgeon if you faint in the operating theatre!

"You should go to hospital," I said to Bethany.

She hadn't even asked what we were doing there. She seemed to be concentrating pretty hard just on dealing with the pain. "I'll be fine," she said tightly and tried to stand up.

"Whoa!" I caught her arm as she fell sideways.

She slumped back on to the sand. "Can someone fetch my stuff?" she said weakly. "It's over there." And she flapped a hand towards where Jude was standing. "The green bag with a yellow stripe…"

"I see it!" said Frankie and raced to get it.

In a minute, Frankie was back. Bethany said, "I'll tie my sweatshirt round my leg," and grabbed the bag, rummaging through it with trembling hands.

Frankie nodded in the direction of Jude and his mates and whispered to me, "They asked if they could help. I said no – right?"

"Right," I agreed. But to be honest, I was worried. "Bethany, you should…" I wanted to say it again.

"The hospital?" Bethany nodded. "Maybe you're right."

"We could ring for an ambulance," said Frankie eagerly.

Lyndz had turned away from the blood and was scanning the beach. "I reckon there's a phone box over there," she said, pointing back the way we'd come. "Or do you have a mobile?"

Gingerly, and with a lot of wincing, Bethany was wrapping her sweatshirt round her leg.

Without looking up, she said, "I do… but you can't get a signal at this end of the beach. There's – there's a phone box down by the place that sells ice creams." She leant back on her hands for a moment, looking at me. She'd gone very pale. "But listen, don't ring the hospital," she said. "Ring Aidan, will you? He'll be at the hostel."

"What's the number?"

Rosie found a pen in her bag and, as Bethany recited the telephone number, I wrote it on my hand. Then all of us except Bethany looked in our purses for ten pence pieces.

"Stay there!" I commanded, tipping a handful of change into my pocket. "I won't be a sec!" And I set off across the beach, running as fast as I could.

As I reached the phone box, I suddenly worried that it'd be out of order. But I was lucky. I picked up the receiver and dialled the number. "Come on, come on," I whispered.

After what seemed like an age, there was a

clunk and Aidan's voice said, "Beach Road Hostel, hello?"

"Aidan, it's Kenny," I gabbled. "Bethany's had an accident. You've got to come…"

In a second I'd told him what had happened and where we were, and he was on his way.

I dashed back across the sand. "He's coming in the car," I panted when I reached the others. "He'll be here really soon. Bethany – you should raise your leg up, I think. Lean it on me." And I knelt down in front of her again.

Lyndz found a towel in Bethany's bag and rolled it into a pillow for her. Bethany lay back. "Thank you," she said and tried to smile.

Soon Rosie, who'd run back to the pathway for a better view of the road, yelled out, "I can see him!" She started jumping up and down, waving her hands above her head.

A minute later, the battered car I remembered from the night of our midnight feast lumbered into view. Aidan had turned off the road and was bumping over the grass, getting as near to the beach as he possibly could.

He stopped not far from where we'd been sitting when we saw the accident, sprang out of the car and, without even stopping to shut the door, sprinted down on to the beach.

As he reached us, I saw him catch sight of the red-stained sweatshirt and swallow, hard. "Bethy, are you all right?" he said, kneeling beside her.

"Been better," said Bethany, giving him a lopsided grin.

"What happened? It was Jude, was it?"

"How about I tell you on the way to the Princess Margaret?"

That must have been the name of the hospital.

Aidan nodded. "It's a deal. Stick your arm round my neck. I'll carry you to the car."

He crouched beside her, putting one arm round her waist and wriggling the other, carefully, under her knees. "Bet you anything it was no accident," he said, as he picked her up.

"Jude wants you out of tomorrow's competition, you know that, don't you? He's scared you might beat him."

"Well, no chance of that now," said Bethany. Then she looked at us over Aidan's shoulder. "Thanks so much, guys, you really helped – I'll see you later!" And with that, they set off across the beach.

I wanted to go too. Wouldn't you? (Well, maybe not – unless you find hospitals as fascinating as I do!) But as I made to follow them, Frankie grabbed my arm.

"Kenny – we're supposed to be at the barbecue," she said.

"What? That's not for ages…" I looked at my watch. And did a massive double take. I'd thought it was about 4 o'clock – 4.30 max. But my watch said 6.15! Mrs Weaver had told us that everyone *had* to be at the barbecue by 6 o'clock at the very latest.

"Oh no, we'd better run for it," I said. "Come on – last one there has to sit with the M&Ms!"

The barbecue was being held at the opposite end of the beach, in a little sheltered cove not far from where Aidan had held his volleyball lessons earlier in the week. It took us a while to get there; although we set off at a dash, Fliss got a stitch about halfway, so we had to slow down. When we finally arrived at the cove, it was clear that we were the last. The rest of the class had already built a rather wonky stone barbecue, and Regina Hill and Ryan Scott were busy trying to light a fire under it.

"Here they are," I heard Miss Walsh say, tapping Mrs Weaver on the shoulder and nodding in our direction.

Mrs Weaver turned. "What time do you girls call this?" she snapped as she strode over to us, her hands on her hips.

"We're ever so sorry," said Rosie. "We didn't realise how late it was – we got so wrapped up in the questionnaire."

I winced. What if Weaver asked to look at our answer sheet? We'd only filled in about two of the blanks.

Luckily, just at that moment, Mrs Daniels came up.

"I can't think where Bethany and Aidan have got to, Mrs Weaver," she said. (Isn't it weird when teachers call each other 'Mrs This' and 'Miss That' just because you're listening? We all know full well they call each other 'Sue' or 'Trish' or whatever in the staffroom.)

Mrs Weaver checked her watch. "Hmm. They're usually so reliable."

"Um, excuse me – Mrs Daniels?" I heard Frankie say before I could stop her. "Bethany had an accident, so Aidan's taken her to the hospital."

"Really?" Mrs Daniels looked concerned. "What kind of an accident?"

"A surfing accident," Frankie replied. "She got a really bad gash on her shin and there was loads of blood, and..."

"How do you know?" Mrs Weaver cut in sharply.

I wanted to put my t-shirt over my head. We were really going to be for it, now!

Frankie hadn't cottoned on. "Oh, we saw it happen!" she was saying. "There was a crash with another surfer…"

"Francesca Thomas, what on *earth* were you doing on the beach?" shouted Mrs Weaver, going bright red in the face and looking as if she was about to explode. "Did I not say that it was absolutely forbidden?"

The whole class went quiet and turned to look at us.

"But we weren't *on* the beach, Mrs Weaver," Frankie protested. "We remembered what you said and we were really careful to keep off it. We stuck to the pathway on the grass – honestly! Until we saw that Bethany was hurt – and that was an emergency. We couldn't leave her bleeding there just because you'd told us…"

145

"That's enough." Mrs Weaver held up her hand. "I will ask Bethany when I see her to give me an account of your behaviour."

"Kenny – I mean, Laura, was going to ring for an ambulance," said Frankie more quietly. "But Bethany said to ring for Aidan instead. It's thanks to her that Bethany got to the hospital so quickly."

"Yes, well…" Mrs Weaver looked from one to the other of us, clearly not sure whether she should be angry or not. "How badly is Bethany hurt?"

"I think she'll be OK," I said, trying to sound like my dad in serious doctor mode. "But she might need stitches."

"Phew! That was a close thing," said Rosie as Mrs Weaver went back to the barbecue. "I thought she was going to put us on the first train home!"

"I know. Talk about over-reacting," Frankie agreed. "Come on – let's find a job that needs doing."

146

The barbecue turned out to be really good fun. We were doing it Robinson Crusoe style: no high-tech equipment like I've seen round at Fliss's house (her mum's boyfriend, Andy, loves barbecues and has all the gadgets). Instead, people were busy spiking sausages on a load of sticks that Ryan and Danny had collected, and holding them over the fire. There were burgers cooking too, and Miss Walsh was trying to barbecue sardines, although they kept falling apart. For the veggies there were corncobs and kebabs made up of pieces of onion, mushroom and green and red peppers, singeing at the edges.

The Sleepover Club volunteered for pudding duty: we peeled a load of bananas, cut a slit in them lengthways and pressed chunks of chocolate and marshmallows into the gap. Then we wrapped them in tin foil so they could be put on the barbecue. Yum, yum, *yum*!

"You know, it's weird, but I had a feeling something bad was going to happen," I said three-quarters of an hour later as we sat on the sand, munching happily.

"Maybe you're psychic!" said Fliss excitedly.

"Always hoping for a medical emergency, more like," laughed Frankie, licking ketchup off her wrist.

"Hey!" said Lyndz. "Look who's here!"

The rest of us turned. Two people were picking their way slowly towards us over the rocks that sheltered the cove from the rest of the beach.

"Aidan and Bethany!" squealed Rosie and Fliss together.

Bethany was on crutches, which made getting over the rocks majorly tricky. She had a pretty hefty bandage on her right leg too.

"Want me to carry you again?" we heard Aidan say, as he waited for her to catch him up.

"Not likely," laughed Bethany. "This is great training. I'm improving my balance, co-ordination, arm strength..."

The teachers hurried over to talk to

148

Bethany as she settled down to sit on a rock, and Aidan came to investigate whether we'd left them any food.

"All's well," he said to us as Frankie handed him a couple of fresh kebabs. "Just one thing: don't cheer for Jude in the competition tomorrow, will you?"

He didn't need to worry. There was no fear of *that*.

10

"What shall I wear? What shall I wear?"

In unison, four voices chorused, "*Anything*!!"

Can you believe we were going through this again?! Fliss had decided she had to wear something special to the Surfing Display Day, which meant – apparently – that she had to try on every single thing she had in her suitcase.

"Come on! We have to be downstairs in two minutes!" I waved my watch under Fliss's nose and bounced off towards the window. I was so excited, I had the jitters and keeping still was not an option.

"One cloud. Small. White," reported Frankie, leaning out of the window. "Don't forget your sunglasses, ladies! It's going to be *hot, hot, hot!*"

I couldn't believe this was our last day in Rawnston. And I couldn't believe we were going to spend it on the beach, watching some seriously cool surfing, and cheering for Aidan till we lost our voices. I couldn't *wait*.

As usual, the whole class walked down to the beach together. You could hear the beach before you could see it: someone had set up a sound system and happy, bouncy music was drifting on the warm, sea-salty breeze.

"Wow! A few people've turned out, then," said Rosie as we turned the corner at the end of the road and the seafront came into view.

Understatement of the year. The beach was heaving. I reckon every single one of the teenagers we'd seen in those cafés and surf shops had come along, and half of them had brought a

151

crowd of mates too. Added to that, there were plenty of other people who didn't look like surfers, plus quite a few kids running around. It seemed as if Aidan's plan for getting the non-surfers of Rawnston interested had paid off.

"Bouncy castle!" exclaimed Lyndz, pointing. "My little brothers would love this!"

"Ice-cream van!" said Frankie, pointing too. "Never mind little brothers – *I* love this!"

Stalls were dotted about, selling all sorts of different things: hot pancakes, cool drinks, surfing magazines, clothes, even surf-themed jewellery – pendants and ear-rings in the shape of surfboards.

"You'd have to be, like, really *obsessed* to wear this stuff," said Fliss, nosing through it.

A friendly girl called Kelly was offering to plait beads and little coloured ribbons into people's hair. "Cool!" yelped Rosie and plumped herself down in front of Kelly's mirror. "C'mon, Kenny, you too!"

"No fear," I said backing away. Don't ask me

why, but I can't stand people fiddling with my hair. Instead, I hurried over to the Surfers For Clean Water petition and queued up to sign it.

When we were done, Frankie pulled out her camera. "I need someone to take a picture, so we can all be in it," she said.

Suddenly, a voice behind us said, "Can I help?"

We spun round. It was Bethany, leaning on her crutches and grinning at us.

We nearly knocked her over by all trying to hug her at once. After yesterday's drama, it felt like she was one of our best friends.

"Hey, careful, guys!" she laughed. "Sprained ankle, remember!"

She took several snaps of us striking silly poses. Then Rosie asked, "When does the surfing competition start?"

Bethany checked her watch. "Any minute now. Want to come and watch with me?"

You bet we did! Bethany led us to a good vantage point and we sat down near a crowd of her friends.

153

"How cool is this?" whispered Frankie to me. "I hope the M&Ms spot us!"

The kids' competition came first. I'd thought the contestants might just do a few simple moves, like the ones we'd learnt this week. Boy, was I wrong. Every single one of them stood up on the board like it was the easiest thing in the world, and then twisted and turned along the wave like a skateboarder.

"That's incredible," said Lyndz, who'd been watching with her mouth open.

"But… they only look a bit older than us," said Rosie.

Bethany nodded. "Remember, though – they live round here and they've been surfing for years already." She nudged Rosie. "You could be like that if you practised hard." Rosie beamed.

If the kids were that good, I wondered what the grown-up competition was going to be like. I could see Aidan standing ready with his board, and not far from him, in the middle of a huddle of friends, I spotted Jude.

"We're supporting Aidan," I told Bethany. "D'you reckon he'll win?"

Bethany pursed her lips, thinking. "Aidan's good," she said. "But, to be honest, Jude is better."

None of us spoke. We didn't want to believe it.

"Always depends what happens on the day, though," Bethany added. "Surfing can be so unpredictable – you're affected by the wind, the waves, the guy you're surfing against..."

"I wish *you* were surfing," Fliss cut in. "We'd be cheering for you!"

"You're my team!" Bethany held up her hand and did high-fives with each of us in turn. At this rate, I thought, we were going to have to make her an honorary member of the Sleepover Club!

Soon the adult competition started and that grabbed all our attention. The format was different from the kids' competition. Then, the contestants had surfed in heats of four and the best from each heat had gone on to the grand final. Now, the surfers were going out in pairs. One from each pair went on to the next round.

"It's really tactical," Bethany explained. "The waves aren't all the same size, of course. And you can only take off – you know, get going on a new wave – ten times; after that you have to come out of the water. So everyone wants to get the best waves for themselves – the ones they're going to be able to perform their favourite moves on."

It was dead exciting seeing really good surfers trying to outdo one another. Before today, we hadn't ever seen Aidan surfing, so when his turn came in the first round I was really interested to check out his skills. And he was majorly impressive. The water sprayed and swooshed as his board sliced across it, and at one point he even jumped into the air, taking his board with him!

"Yeeaahh! Go, Aidan!" we cheered. And when it was announced that he'd got through to the second round, we cheered even harder.

156

Next, though, he was going to be pitted against Jude.

"This'll be a tough one," said Bethany. "Jude is a mean competitor."

Somehow, I wasn't surprised.

When the time came and they waded out into the water together, we all watched with bated breath. Aidan had won the toss, which meant that he had first pick of which wave to take off on. I was hoping that would give him a major advantage.

After paddling out and sitting up on his board for a while, waiting for the bigger waves, Aidan turned his board around. He was off!

From our vantage point on the sand, the six of us watched intently. Aidan rode the wave, turning at the bottom, swooshing up to the top and cutting back again. He looked so good – but I kept glancing at Bethany. I wanted to know how *she* thought it was going.

Bethany was biting her lip. A little later I saw her check her watch.

"They've got twenty minutes in total," she explained. "Ade's had the best waves so far, but Jude can pull out some radical moves under pressure. I should know – he's beaten me that way."

The crowd around us was whistling and cheering – I tried to judge by the noises they made which moves were the best. Everything looked impressive to me. At one point, Jude got right under the curl of a wave and leaned back into the wall of water, trailing his hand across it. It was *awesome*.

"Whoever wins this heat's gonna win the whole competition, I reckon," I heard someone say nearby. And it turned out that they were right.

So, who won? Shall I give you three guesses? Yep, it was Jude, I'm afraid. And however much we didn't like him, we had to admit that his surfing had been pretty gobsmacking.

A man with a microphone did the presentation – the prize was a wad of vouchers for a surf shop and a bottle of champagne. After that, we watched as Bethany went to congratulate Aidan. Jude spotted her and tried to talk to her, but she gave him the cold shoulder.

"Too right," said Frankie, nodding approvingly. "I hope he's feeling really guilty."

"He should give her the vouchers he's won," said Rosie. "And the champagne."

"One of us ought to go and tell him," said Lyndz.

Silence. No one moved. We were all just staring at Jude and his smug-looking friends.

"Well, when someone's that bigheaded, it's probably better just to ignore them," suggested Fliss.

"Absolutely." Frankie, Lyndz and Rosie nodded quickly.

Slowly, I got to my feet. I had made it into that scary café the other day. After that, how could Kenny McKenzie, brave Leicester City supporter and founder member of the glorious Sleepover Club, be frightened of some weedy, puff-headed surf boy?

Never mind *how*. I could. I was.

But I wasn't going to let that stop me.

Heels digging into the sand, I marched across to where Jude was crouching, putting something into his bag.

"Excuse me," I said when I got there. Somehow, it came out a bit squeaky. I cleared my throat and repeated it, more loudly.

Jude looked up. "Yes? Who are you?" He frowned. "Oh, I know," he said, "you're one of those babies Bethany's been teaching."

I wasn't going to let his sneering put me off. "We know the accident was your fault," I said, staring him right in the eye. "You did it because you were scared of Bethany beating you. We think you're a coward and you should give the prizes you won to Bethany."

I stood there, breathing hard, my heart thumping so loudly I thought everyone must be able to hear it.

For a moment, Jude looked completely blank. Then he started to laugh. At that moment, one of his friends came up. "Munchkin trouble, Jude?" he said, looking at me like I was a manky bit of seaweed that the tide had left behind.

Jude shrugged. "Oh, you know how I *love* the little darlings," he said. And he reached out a hand and ruffled my hair.

He ruffled my hair. I told you I couldn't stand anyone fiddling with my barnet, didn't I? Well, this was the last straw. I was just about to go for him, *really* go for him – practise my kung fu kick and my karate chop, when Frankie suddenly appeared at my side and said, "C'mon, Kenny. Forget these losers – Bethany said she'd buy us all pancakes!"

I would've got him. I would've had him begging for mercy. Honestly. But... pancakes? Hot pancakes with melted chocolate and vanilla ice cream inside? No contest! Giggling like crazy, I turned and raced with Frankie across the beach.

I wasn't disappointed, either: the pancakes

161

were de*lish*. But the reaction of my friends was even better. Never mind that Jude wasn't going to hand over his prizes to anyone in a million years, they still made me feel like I'd just saved an entire city from an evil super-villain.

"Wow, you were so brave!" said Rosie, looking at me with wide eyes. "The way you just went up to him – it was awesome!"

"You told him!" said Lyndz. "You didn't let him get away with it! You gave him a piece of your mind!"

"It was heroic!" said Frankie, grinning a chocolatey grin and clapping me on the shoulder.

"Well, maybe just a bit," I admitted modestly. "And you know what? Dealing with the M&Ms'll feel like *nothing* after Rude Jude!"

I was right. We've been back in Cuddington for almost two weeks now and the M&Ms have barely registered on my radar. For one thing,

I've been too busy plotting how to get Mum and Dad to change their plans for our summer holiday. We just *have* to go somewhere where I can catch some surf. I've even threatened to start practising on the ironing board!

And it's not just me. Every member of the Sleepover Club has been having serious withdrawal symptoms since we left Rawnston. Rosie's determined that we're going to be the first surf-dudes ever to be based in Leicestershire – but boy, do I wish that we could wave a magic wand and turn Cuddington into Cuddington-on-Sea! That's why I invited everyone round to mine today, in fact, to hang out in the garden and pretend that all this grass is actually golden sand...

Oops – have you seen the time? I can't believe we've been gassing so long! Listen, I'd better go and fix everyone some drinks in a sec or I'll have a gang of parched sunbathers giving me a hard time. But I must just tell you one more thing: we got a postcard from

Bethany the other day. (She sent it to us at school, cos she didn't have our home addresses.) She wanted to let us know that her leg had healed. And she mentioned – just dropped it in – that she and Jude are good friends now. I mean... how completely *weird* is that? Don't you think? We've all talked about it loads, of course, and it's Aidan we feel sorry for. Fliss thinks he's in *lurve* with Bethany, but that's Fliss for you – it's all those soppy films she watches.

Oh help! That's Frankie now, yelling for lemonade! Tell her to keep her hair on, will you? I've got to run. Catch you later. Byeeee!

Kenny's Beach Picnic Treats

Hi everyone!
Here are my fave
recipes for chilling out
on a hot summer's day...
Kenny xx

Homemade Lemonade

You will need:

6 lemons
150g (5oz) granulated sugar

Squeeze the lemon juice into a bowl, (1) removing all pips.

Add the sugar and 2.5 pints of boiling (2) water, stir and let it cool.

Leave in the fridge overnight. (3)

Now you have a refreshing drink for a hot summer's day, or a cool wake-up drink for the morning after a sleepover!

Fruit Kebabs

You will need:

- Wooden skewers
- Pineapple, cut into chunks
- Strawberries
  (whole, with the green stalks removed)
- Mango, cut into chunks
- Grapes, green and red (whole)
- Kiwi fruit, peeled and cut into chunks

(1) Thread the fruit chunks on to the wooden skewers for an outdoor snack in the sun.

(2) Try dipping the strawberries into melted chocolate and refrigerate on sheets of greaseproof paper before adding them to the kebab. Yum.

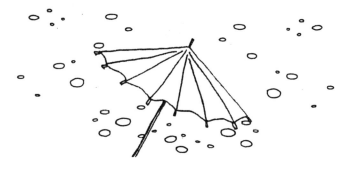

Summer Berry Crush

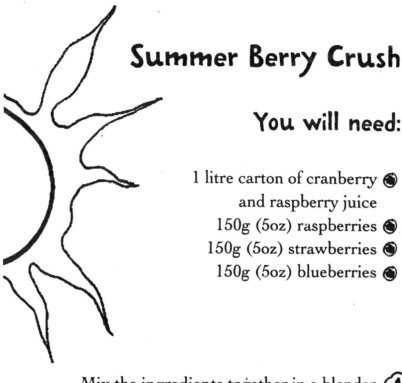

You will need:

1 litre carton of cranberry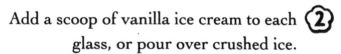
and raspberry juice
150g (5oz) raspberries
150g (5oz) strawberries
150g (5oz) blueberries

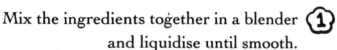
Mix the ingredients together in a blender **(1)**
and liquidise until smooth.

Add a scoop of vanilla ice cream to each **(2)**
glass, or pour over crushed ice.

Fliss's Funky Flip-flops

Bored with your plain
old flip-flops? Why
not jazz them up for
your sleepover?

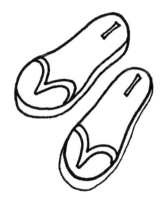

You will need:

- Plain flip-flops
- Buttons, sequins, rhinestones, bows
  (anything small and pretty)
- Adhesive craft pads or double-sided
  sticky tape

1. Work out a pretty design using the
   buttons, or whatever you can find.

2. Use the pads/sticky tape to attach them
   to the strappy part of your flip-flops!

FLISS ✗

Have your own summer sleepover, whatever the weather!

(1) Bring bathing suits, sarongs, sunglasses and flip-flops and get dressed up.

(2) Make Kenny's refreshing picnic treats.

(3) Blow up a balloon, split into two teams and stand facing each other on either side of the room. Play indoor beach volleyball. Watch the ornaments!

Have a brilliant time at your own sleepovers, whatever you do! See you next time – for another purrrfect sleepover story...

Kenny x

Coming soon!

You are invited to join Frankie, Lyndz, Kenny, Rosie and me on our next Sleepover Club mission in...

The SleePover Club

Pet Detectives

Lyndz's gorgeous cat Truffle has gone missing, but we're determined to track her down. It's time to go undercover...

Shhh... don't let the cat out of the bag - just come along and

join the club!

From

FLiSS ✗

YOU are invited to join Lyndz, Kenny, Fliss, Rosie and me for our first Sleepover Club story in...

The Sleepover Club

Best Friends!

Want to know how we all became friends, had our first sleepover and formed the Best Club in the World Ever!

Come on! What are **you** waiting for? **Join the club!**

From

Frankie x

YOU are invited to join Frankie, Lyndz, Fliss, Kenny and me for our next sleepover in...

The SleePover Club

Dance-Off!

The Sleepover Babes are on a mission to win the school dance competition - no way are we letting our enemies, the M&Ms, dance all over us!

Have **you** got some funky moves? Come along and join the club!

From

Rosie x

Lightning Source UK Ltd.
Milton Keynes UK
15 May 2010

154240UK00001B/3/P

9 780007 272563